"Maybe you need a husband."

A what now?

Thatcher's attempt to lighten the mood by making a goofy joke wasn't funny. He had no way of knowing how unhappy Bliss's marriage was, though, so she tried to keep her tone light. "If you're trying to be humorous, stick to knock-knock jokes."

"I'm serious." Thatcher's stare was so intense, he didn't even blink. "Marriage could solve some of your problems immediately."

"And create a heap more." She'd already had a husband, and he'd left her with nothing. "I heard about Beatie and Dutch playing matchmaker with Sadie and Mick, but I didn't expect it from you, too. I'll make it clear—I'm not interested. Now, I'm going to take this salad out to the dining room and we can forget this conversation ever happened." She gathered the glass bowl of salad and turned away.

"It's me."

She stopped. Then turned around to face him. "What did you say?"

He looked her straight in the eye, his cocoa-dark eyes soft. "You could marry me, Bliss."

Susanne Dietze began writing love stories in high school, casting her friends in the starring roles. Today, she's an award-winning, RWA RITA® Award–nominated author who's seen her work on the ECPA and *Publishers Weekly* bestseller lists for inspirational fiction. Married to a pastor and a mom of two, Susanne lives in California and enjoys fancy-schmancy tea parties, the beach and curling up on the couch with a costume drama. To learn more, say hi or sign up for her newsletter, visit her website, www.susannedietze.com.

Books by Susanne Dietze

Love Inspired

Home to Foxtail

Mountain Homecoming
Her Pretend Holiday Beau
A Rancher for Easter

Widow's Peak Creek

A Future for His Twins
Seeking Sanctuary
A Small-Town Christmas Challenge
A Need to Protect
The Secret Between Them

Love Inspired Historical

The Reluctant Guardian
A Mother for His Family

Visit the Author Profile page at LoveInspired.com.

A RANCHER FOR EASTER

SUSANNE DIETZE

Recycling programs for this product may not exist in your area.

ISBN-13: 978-1-335-62148-1

A Rancher for Easter

For questions and comments about the quality of this book, please contact us at CustomerService@Harlequin.com.

Love Inspired
22 Adelaide St. West, 41st Floor
Toronto, Ontario M5H 4E3, Canada
www.LoveInspired.com

HarperCollins Publishers
Macken House, 39/40 Mayor Street Upper,
Dublin 1, D01 C9W8, Ireland
www.HarperCollins.com

Printed in Lithuania

Behold, what manner of love the Father hath bestowed upon us, that we should be called the sons of God: therefore the world knoweth us not, because it knew him not.

—*1 John* 3:1

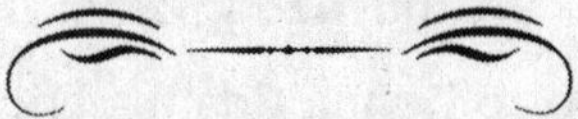

In loving memory of Samantha Chaffee.

Swallowtail butterflies are everywhere this year, Sam—sunny and free, and oh, how they remind me of you. We miss you, sweet girl.

Acknowledgments:

Special thanks to Donna Chaffee and Andi Tubbs, who answered my questions about service dogs and epilepsy with patience and kindness. Any errors in the manuscript are mine, however.

Thanks, too, to my gifted editor, Amanda Sun; to my generous agent, Tamela Hancock Murray; to my patient, hilarious family; and to Jesus, who has never let us go from His hand.

Chapter One

You're not being paid to be nosy.

Resolving to mind her own business, Bliss Anderson forced her gaze back to the spreadsheet on the computer monitor. Where had she been before she was distracted? Oh, yes. The receipt for supplemental cattle feed.

Movement outside Foxtail Ranch's office caught her attention again, and despite her best intentions, she watched Thatcher Dalton pace in front of the window. He scowled, his phone to his ear as he shook his head. Then he paused in place and looked skyward, shutting his eyes.

Was he getting bad news?

She resisted the urge to rush outside to him. It wasn't her place.

Keep your eyes on the work the Daltons pay you to do. Give the man his privacy until—unless—he decides to confide in you.

But how could she not notice Thatcher? The man was impossible to ignore even when he wasn't stomping back and forth in her direct line of sight. Six foot two, his muscular frame honed by hard work on the ranch, Thatcher was an imposing figure of a man.

Handsome, too, with his dark wavy hair and chiseled features.

What Bliss liked best about him, though, was the way his cocoa brown eyes were always full of laughter.

Almost always, anyway. He clearly wasn't laughing now.

Bliss returned to the spreadsheet and tapped in the total spent on additional feed, praying for Thatcher at the same time. He might be a client of the bookkeeping firm she worked for, but he was also her neighbor and friend, and he was clearly upset.

"I'm stuck on this one. Would you help me, please?" Juniper Jones, Bliss's nine-year old foster daughter, shoved a math page between Bliss and the computer monitor.

Bliss had been so engrossed in observing Thatcher that she hadn't registered the freckled fourth grader leaving the spare office chair. Nor did Bliss register that Coco, Juniper's black Labrador service dog, had accompanied her, and Coco wasn't exactly quiet when she moved. Not with her toes tippy-tapping on the linoleum floor.

"Sure, sweet girl. Let's see what we're dealing with." Bliss took the paper of long division problems.

"This one." Juniper pointed with her right hand, setting off a faint chorus of metallic tinkling as her charm bracelet tapped against her silver medical alert band.

Bliss looked over the problem. "Double-digit divisors are tricky."

"Tell me about it."

Bliss wrapped an arm around Juniper's slender frame while she explained the method for solving the problem, grateful Thatcher was so easygoing that he hadn't batted an eye when she asked to bring Juniper and Coco along with her today. Fridays in January were not usually school holidays, but this last Friday of the month was one of those in-service days when the teachers had meetings and the kids got a day off. Since Bliss's usual sitter was out of commission with strep throat, Bliss had been in a bind this morning. Thankfully, the Dalton family who ran Foxtail Farm and Ranch didn't mind kids or dogs.

The four Daltons—Thatcher and his three cousins, sisters Natalie, Sadie and Dove—had inherited Foxtail Farm three years ago from the women's father, Asa Dalton, but the gift wasn't straightforward. Asa's will stated that Thatcher and his cousins had to live and work at the Foxtail property for five years, changing nothing in the way the "U-Pick" apple orchard, farmstand, bakery or adjacent ranch, which Thatcher ran, were operated. If one of the Daltons failed, the farm and ranch would be sold, the employees let go, and each Dalton would lose his or her inheritance.

Some changes had occurred the past three years, of course, but they were all in accordance with Asa's will. Bliss admired every effort the Daltons made to keep Foxtail Farm afloat despite the limitations on them. They were good people, and she had become friends with all four Daltons since her employer, Berg Bookkeeping Services, had assigned her to Foxtail Farm's accounts.

Her job wasn't perfect, especially considering Gunther Berg's cold demeanor, but her work allowed her to live comfortably in the house her grandpa had left to her in her hometown of Goldenrod, a small town nestled in California's Cuyamaca Mountains. The job's flexibility also enabled her to work from home most afternoons so she could be with Juniper, whom she was in the process of adopting.

Juniper scrawled on her math page, leaning against Bliss's chair. "Like this?"

"Perfect. I'll be done with my work here in ten minutes or so. Then we can visit Miss Dove at the bakery before we go to the birthday barbecue, okay?"

"Sure." Juniper curled back into the chair with her notebook on her lap. Coco, ever mindful of her role to assist Juniper in the event of an epileptic seizure, lay at her feet. It was a wise choice, since it was close to the floor vent. The heat was welcome on such a chilly day.

So chilly Bliss wondered if Thatcher was going to turn into a human popsicle if he stayed outside much longer. When he'd rushed outside to take the phone call, he hadn't put on a coat over his well-worn jeans and her favorite of his flannel shirts, a dark blue plaid.

Not that she should have favorites of his clothes. She was not interested in Thatcher. He was a good guy, no question, and a far cry from the men she used to have in her life. She was grateful for the presence of decent, godly men around Juniper, too.

But that didn't mean she was open to dating. Juniper was her top priority. Maybe someday, if a special guy appeared, ready to commit to them as a package deal, she might consider it. A long, long time from now.

She puffed out a sigh. If she was actually going to finish up with Foxtail Ranch's expenses, as she'd told Juniper, she had better focus on the task at hand.

She snuck one more glance at Thatcher, because his left arm flung up in the air like a bull rider trying to regain balance.

You know what's causing him such concern, Lord, and I ask You to help him. Bliss lowered her head so it would be harder for her to stare out the window. *And forgive me for being such a snoop.*

A few minutes later, she tapped the computer mouse, and with a click and a whir, the old printer on Thatcher's scratched desk came to life. The paper spat out, and she tucked it into a manila folder for Foxtail Farm's next office meeting.

As she saved the document, her phone vibrated against the desk. Gunther Berg's name scrolled across the screen. He wasn't a big texter, but he often called when she was with clients to request an additional task like picking up paperwork or making a deposit.

She answered quickly. "Hi, Gunther."

"Are you still at Foxtail Farm?" His nasal tone sounded especially pinched today.

"Yes—the ranch, to be precise. I'm finishing up now. Do you need me to make another stop?"

"Just back to the office, if you don't mind."

She hated to disappoint Juniper, after telling her they could visit Foxtail's bakery to kill some time until tonight's barbecue started, but she couldn't say no to Gunther. "I'll be there shortly."

He hung up before she could mention Juniper would be with her. Hopefully he would understand.

Thatcher came back inside, accompanied by a frigid gust of air. He grinned at Juniper, but the smile didn't reach his eyes. "How's math treating you, Junie?"

Juniper shoved her pencil into the pale blue backpack at her feet. "Better now that Bliss helped."

"What can I say?" Bliss shut down her laptop. "Math is my thing." Sort of. She was no scholar, just someone who liked figures and formulas enough to make a living at it.

No matter how incapable her late husband Lane and his family said she was.

"Speaking of math." There was no trace of displeasure on Thatcher's face, other than the noticeable lack of spark in his eyes. "Knock, knock, Juniper."

"Here we go." Bliss mentally buckled herself in for a joke-a-thon, one of Juniper and Thatcher's favorite pastimes whenever they were together.

"Who's there, Mr. Thatcher?" Juniper retorted.

Thatcher rubbed the faint stubble on his jaw. "Math."

"Math who?"

"Can you pass the math potatoes and gravy?" Thatcher rubbed his lean stomach. "I'm hungry."

Juniper giggled. "Me, too, but we get to go to Miss Dove's bakery now."

"Change of plans, Juniper." Bliss slipped her laptop into her satchel-style purse. "Mr. Berg asked me to drop into the office. I'm so sorry, but we'll get a treat after that."

"Aw. I wanted to see Miss Dove." Juniper snapped the purple silicone bracelet for epilepsy awareness that she wore on her left wrist. "Well, I guess we'll see her tonight at Dr. Mick's party, anyway."

Thatcher held out Juniper's coat, helping her into it. His consideration toward Bliss's foster daughter, even when he was clearly going through something unpleasant, proved what a good heart he had. "I have to run downtown, too, so why don't I give you two a ride there and back? Saves gasoline."

"Are you sure it wouldn't be any trouble?" Berg Bookkeeping was located just off the main drag through their historic town. The street boasted several shops, but none were the kind that sold farm supplies. It was hard to picture him in any other type of store.

"That's right where I'm going. Sadie just texted, and she's a few doors down from Berg's picking up a present for Mick."

His cousin Sadie was a florist who ran the Foxtail farmstand, and Mick, a veterinarian whose birthday they were celebrating, was her new fiancé. "The battery in her minivan died, so she asked me to swing by for a jump. She can't reach out to Mick for help, because then he'll know where she is, and it would ruin the surprise of the present. Or something along those lines. Anyway, Juniper can hang out with us while you talk to Gunther."

If Sadie had texted, rather than called, then she couldn't have been the person on the phone who had caused Thatcher so much grief just now. Curiosity burned, but Bliss once again tried to shift her concern into action by sending a brief prayer heavenward before answering Thatcher. "That would be amazing. Is that okay with you, Juniper?"

"It sounds fun." Juniper gathered her backpack, as well as the hot-pink bag that carried Coco's water bottle and snacks. "Miss Sadie is so nice, and she loves Coco."

Coco responded to this pronouncement by wagging her tail.

"We all do. She's a good girl. Aren't you, Coke?" Thatcher rubbed Coco's forehead, then shrugged into a buff utility jacket. "Ready?"

Bliss fastened the royal blue service vest Coco wore in public around the dog's chest. "Yep. Let's go."

Fortunately, he had an extended cab truck, so there was plenty of room for them all. A few years old, the gray vehicle seemed to represent Thatcher well in Bliss's opinion: a few small scratches and a bed full of toolboxes testified to his hard work, but it was nevertheless so clean that even the license plate holder declaring Thatcher a member of the Gallon Club at the blood bank sparkled in the winter sunlight. A white Foxtail Ranch logo decal was the only other personalization on the exterior, but inside, there was no mistaking whose vehicle it was. It smelled like him—earth, cedar and a faint whiff of laundry detergent.

Juniper and Coco piled into the back seat, and after Bliss buckled up, she twisted to make sure they were secure, too.

Thatcher started the engine. The radio was set to a country music station and he turned it down, then the heater up. "We'll be toasty in no time."

His tone was cheery, but his fingers gripped the steering wheel as he turned onto the curvy, two-lane road that led to the historic heart of town. Once, the village in the pines had been known for its gold mine, but now, Goldenrod was a charming tourist stop, home to several small ranches and apple orchards, like Foxtail Farm.

Were those other businesses thriving more than Foxtail Farm and Ranch were? As Foxtail's bookkeeper, Bliss knew a lot of private details about Foxtail's enterprises...and the Daltons themselves. Sometimes, she was handed envelopes they had confused for bills based on the return addresses. Once, Bliss had seen an appointment summary from Natalie's twin toddlers' doctor visits, and she'd also opened a letter thanking Thatcher for donating his AB blood—not that she hadn't already figured he was a blood donor after seeing his license plate holder.

But because she handled the family's accounts, she also knew how tight their finances were. Especially considering they were managing under the strict conditions laid out in Asa Dalton's will.

Bliss had never met the man, but based on his actions, she had a good idea what Asa must have been like. She knew a thing or two about controlling men, those who enjoyed playing puppet master with vulnerable people.

She thought she had escaped that sort of life when she'd left home and her domineering dad, only to realize she'd jumped from the frying pan into the fire by marrying Lane Anderson—Bliss shook her head at herself. What was wrong with her, thinking about her marriage right now? There were far more pressing matters at hand. Like whatever was upsetting Thatcher so much that a muscle bulged in his cheek as if he were clenching his jaw.

All she could do was pray as Juniper peppered Thatcher with knock-knock jokes from the back seat. *Whatever it is, Lord, Thatcher knows You. Help him to lean on You, and please provide for him.*

And for me, she tacked on. Because Gunther calling her into the office wasn't sitting well on her stomach.

Lord, thanks for Bliss and Juniper being with me in the truck. Thatcher hadn't offered to take them downtown to ensure his temper stayed in check, but their presence was certainly helpful that way. If he were alone, he probably would have given into his simmering anger and sped into town like a Formula One racer.

A foolish act like that could affect himself and others, which was something of a theme in his life today, wasn't it? He had reached out to the estate lawyer this morning with a simple question…and inadvertently triggered a modification to Uncle Asa's will that would alter his life forever.

And by extension, his cousins' lives, too.

Why couldn't Thatcher have kept his mouth shut? Because now, he would lose the ranch in six months unless he—

"Thatcher?" Bliss cut into his reverie. Her voice was soft and gentle, two words that described her in pretty much every way, from her mannerisms to the beige fuzzy sweater she wore beneath her brown coat. With compassionate blue eyes, golden blond hair and a dusting of freckles on her pert nose, she exuded a girl-next-door sweetness.

Not that he had thought of her romantically. But he was grateful they were friends. Good enough friends that if he confided in her right now, she would undoubtedly offer a consoling word and a promise to pray in that gentle way of hers.

But he couldn't tell her what was on his mind. Not with Juniper in the car.

Which reminded him…he sure hoped he hadn't just zoned out during one of the girl's knock-knock jokes. "Sorry, I was lost in thought. What was that?"

"She said it's our song." Bliss pointed to the truck's stereo system. Then her cheeks turned as bright pink as Coco's treat bag. "Not *our* song, I mean, but that song we all like. Remember?"

He did. He, Juniper and Bliss had sung along to the peppy tune a few weeks ago while cleaning up after a church event. He peeked at Juniper through the rearview mirror.

She sat forward, grinning. "Want to sing with me again?"

"I sure do." Anything to make Juniper smile.

Besides, it was better to sing than dwell on the curveball Uncle Asa had thrown him from beyond the grave. Shoving down a fresh wave of ire, he cranked up the volume.

The three of them belted out the lyrics as he drove past lush pines and bare-branched oaks toward downtown. Thatcher's blood pressure felt double digits lower by the time the song ended. He turned the volume down again. "Perfect timing. We're almost there."

"Bliss?" Juniper's high voice came from the back seat. "I forgot I said I'd text Grandma today. Can I have your phone?"

"You may." Bliss scooped the phone from her purse and handed it over her shoulder.

"I wouldn't have to use *your* phone if I had my own." Juniper sounded hopeful.

"Nine years old is too young for your own phone."

"I'll be ten soon."

"True, but ten is still too young." Bliss's patient tone was firm but kind, subtly laced with amusement. "Tell your grandma hello from me."

The conversation between foster mom and daughter made Thatcher smile. He might not ever be a parent himself, but it wasn't because he didn't like kids. He loved them. But being a dad himself?

Not happening.

While Juniper tapped away in the back seat, he glanced at Bliss. "How's Juniper's grandma doing?"

"Vera is well, all things considered."

By *all things*, Thatcher knew Bliss was referring to the lingering effects of the stroke Vera suffered a few years ago, plus back issues that caused debilitating flare-ups. Those struggles had compelled Vera to ask Bliss to foster—and eventually adopt—Juniper.

"I'm praying for her." And he did, every morning before the sun rose, while he spent time with God and a cup of coffee.

He had only attended church for a few years now, but he trusted that God heard him and cared about his needs. Which reminded him—he should be praying about the change he had triggered in Uncle Asa's will. Just thinking about it made his grip tighten on the steering wheel as he turned onto Main Street.

Bliss must have noticed his hands, because she leaned toward him. "Is everything all right?"

There was no way to answer that truthfully now, so he deflected. "Nothing that won't work out one way or another. Here we are." He slid into an empty spot a few doors down from Berg Bookkeeping, right beside a silver minivan with a Foxtail Farm decal on the side. Sadie, bundled in a red coat and knit cap that hid her blond hair, waited on the sidewalk, smiling at them.

"Thanks for the ride." Bliss unbuckled. "I'm not sure how long this could take, but I'll tell Gunther I have to come back for Juniper so you're not waiting long."

Thatcher shut off the engine. "We'll be fine. In fact, you planned to get a treat, right? Is it okay if we grab something while we wait for you?"

"If you're sure you don't mind—"

"I never say no to a doughnut, Bliss. Or spending time with people I care about. So go take care of work. I'll text you to let you know where we end up, and if anything happens, I'll call right away."

And by anything, he meant the unlikely event of Juniper suffering an epileptic seizure.

Bliss's eyes shimmered in understanding. "I appreciate you taking such good care of her, Thatcher. You're a good friend to both of us." Then she turned to the back seat. "Have fun. I love you."

"Love you, too." Juniper scratched Coco's dark ears before getting out.

Bliss hopped out of the cab, stopping to greet Sadie with a brief hug. Thatcher followed her out and retrieved his emergency kit from the truck bed.

When he came back around to the front, he reached for Sadie's keys. "You're sure it's the battery?"

"I hope so, because I don't have time for a big repair right now." Sadie chuckled, but stress lined her eyes and mouth. "There's a lot left to do for Mick's party, but I didn't have a choice. The engraved frame I ordered from Whimsy and Wonders just arrived, and I wanted to give it to him tonight. It's so cute."

"Cute like a bunny rabbit?" Juniper looked wary.

Thatcher held back a snort.

"Not that kind of cute," Sadie was saying as he got into her minivan.

He turned the key in the ignition. *Click click click.* He popped the hood open and got back out.

"Tomorrow, Mick's actual birthday, is National Hot Chocolate Day," Sadie explained to Juniper. "So I ordered an engraved frame that says 'We go together like hot chocolate and marshmallows,' which is an inside joke because Mick hates marshmallows."

That was news to Thatcher. He had half a mind to wrap up a package of marshmallows as a gag gift for his good friend. It would be a funny distraction from his grievances. But right now, he needed to jump-start Sadie's battery.

He looked over at her. "You were right about the battery. This will take a few minutes and then we can grab a treat if Bliss isn't finished yet. What do you want?"

Juniper's features turned shy. "Anything's fine, but when Miss Sadie brought up hot chocolate, it sounded pretty good."

"Sure thing."

"Why don't Juniper and I go to The Bean Machine, and you can meet us when you're done?" Sadie suggested.

Thatcher tugged his wallet from the back pocket of his jeans and tossed it to Sadie. "Great idea."

"Thanks, Mr. Thatcher." Juniper did a little dance. "They give Coco free pup cups."

Hearing that, Coco's excited tail thwacked Thatcher's shin. He bent down to give the dog a brief scratch but didn't linger because Coco was wearing her vest, a signal that she was on duty. He would never want to distract her from her job of paying close attention to Juniper.

"What exactly is in a pup cup?" Sadie waved at Thatcher as she guided Juniper toward the coffee spot down the street. "Whipped cream? Or is there a secret ingredient added just for dogs?"

Thatcher chuckled, then got busy with the jumper cables. The task wasn't enough to hold his full attention, however, and within about thirty seconds he was replaying the conversation he'd had with Uncle Asa's estate lawyer. Not even the bite in the air could cool his temper, which grew hotter by the second.

All Thatcher had wanted to do was make a few adaptations to get through the drought. The price of supplemental feed was draining everything he had. If he could expand the ranch's current borders into the acres of unused Foxtail property—which was literally greener on the other side of the fence, since it was closer to an underground water source—his cattle would have fresh pastures to graze.

Plus, there would be room to grow his own hay. There would be initial costs involved in making these changes, but it wasn't like he would make a profit until he could expand the herd. This was about survival.

There had seemed no harm in asking the lawyer if there was a loophole in Uncle Asa's will to accommodate for such unusual circumstances.

It turned out there was plenty of harm in asking, seeing as how it triggered a shocking proviso that said he had to get married within six months or lose Foxtail Ranch.

Grunting, he glanced at his watch. Twelve minutes had passed since he'd started the process of jumping Sadie's battery. He tapped out a text to Bliss, informing her he was about ready to meet Juniper and Sadie at The Bean Machine and she could join them whenever she was finished with Gunther.

She didn't respond, but that wasn't a shock, considering she was at work. After a few more minutes, he shut off his and Sadie's engines, packed up his cables, locked the cars and strode around the corner to the coffee shop.

Sadie and Juniper sat at a table by the window, mugs of cocoa and a plate of cookie crumbs between them. Coco lounged at Juniper's feet beside a licked-clean pup cup.

He greeted them with a smile. "Hey, ladies. I'm going to get a coffee—"

The woodblock sound he recognized as Bliss's text message alert snicked from the tabletop. Sure enough, Bliss's phone rested atop the table at Juniper's elbow, and there on her screen was his unread text under a text from Bliss's friend Olivia.

Juniper bit her lip. "I still have Bliss's phone from when I was texting Grandma."

"Will she know to look for us here?" Sadie returned Thatcher's wallet to him.

Maybe, but Thatcher didn't want to cause Bliss a moment's uncertainty. "I'll run the phone down to her. Be back in a few." He didn't want to sit still, anyway. What he really wanted was to climb in his truck and drive hard and fast, as far away as he could, until he figured out what to do about Asa's ridiculous will.

He welcomed the cold gust in his face as he strode to Berg's Bookkeeping Services, praying all the while.

I can't get married, God. There has to be a way out of this. Please show me what to do.

But if God had an easy answer, it wasn't obvious to Thatcher right now.

He had to be patient, but it was difficult to imagine how God would help him. It wasn't like a single woman was going to stumble across his path today.

Not one desperate enough to marry a guy like him, anyway.

Chapter Two

Bliss rapped the frame of Gunther's open office door. "My reports are printed. Where would you like them?"

Gunther, a sixty-something fellow with fading blond hair combed over his balding crown, glanced up. With one pudgy finger, he tapped the wooden tray at the corner of his oak desk. "Right here, please."

She set down the manila file folder full of the end-of-month reports. Since today was the last working day of January, Gunther's request for reports made perfect sense, but he usually gave her a few days into the new month to produce them.

It wasn't her place to ask why he wanted them now, however.

"Thank you, Bliss." He continued writing something on a notepad. "I can always count on you to finish your work quickly."

"That's nice to hear." And a surprise, too. Gunther wasn't big on compliments.

"Nevertheless, it is time to part ways."

Surely, she hadn't heard him correctly. "I'm sorry?"

"Effective immediately. You are entitled to a severance package, of course—"

"I'm fired?" Her knees weakening, Bliss gripped the

cane-back chair across from his desk. "What did I do wrong? Please allow me to fix it."

"This isn't about your abilities, as I will state in the glowing reference I will provide for your prospective employers."

"Then why?" Panic clawed at her throat.

He set down his pen, but still didn't look at her. "I'm restructuring."

His words stung, but they were tempered by the understanding that Goldenrod was a small town. Maybe business was dwindling, and it was no longer sustainable to keep her on. "You're going to handle all of the accounts yourself, then?"

"Not quite," Gunther said, dispelling her notion. "My nephew graduated from college in December, and he's ready to join me. I can't employ both of you. It's nothing personal."

It is to me.

Once, she would have accepted the news and, head down, rushed from the room like a quiet mouse.

She was no longer that girl, but speaking up still took more courage than she naturally possessed. She prayed for God's help and took a deep breath.

"Juniper's adoption will be official soon, so I must have employment. You're the only bookkeeping firm in the area. Could we discuss a way to make something work? Please, Gunther. Don't fire me now." Maybe it was unprofessional of her to beg, but—

"Did you say you're fired?"

She spun around. Thatcher filled the doorway, his jaw set, his thick brows drawn low over his eyes. Her pink-cased phone—she'd forgotten she left it with Juniper to text Vera—looked like a toy in his huge, calloused hand.

"Mr. Dalton." Gunther stood. "I assure you, Foxtail will continue to receive the top-quality service you've grown accustomed to. Nothing will change."

"That's right, because Bliss is the only person who does our books." Thatcher's brows drew even lower into an intimidating line.

"That won't be possible." Gunther's face mottled purple, like a ripening plum.

Thatcher stepped closer to the desk. Gunther stepped back as if he were preparing to flee. Not that Thatcher was a violent sort, but his size was intimidating. So was the look in his eyes.

"If Bliss no longer works for you, then you no longer work for Foxtail. We'll hire Bliss as our bookkeeper, without you as the middleman."

Bliss gasped. This might be the first time a man had ever stood up for her. Her father never had, nor had her husband. The strangest sensation spread through her, as if a soothing balm covered some wounded place within her.

Even if his offer was not tenable. "Thatcher, no, it's okay."

His expression softened. "My cousins will agree to bring you on, if that's what you're worried about."

It wasn't, but she didn't want to air her concerns about Foxtail's precarious finances in front of her boss—oops. Former boss. "I'll clear out my things, now, Gunther. Come with me please, Thatcher?"

Thatcher let out a disappointed-sounding sigh, like he would prefer to stay and give Gunther a piece of his mind, but he followed her.

With Thatcher's presence looming large behind her, she gathered her framed photo of Juniper, a box of peach tea and a glittery coaster Juniper had given her for Christmas, scooping them into her big purse after removing the laptop she had been issued on her first day of work here. There were no personal files on it to be cleaned, so she was free to go now.

"Ready."

Thatcher's response was a curt nod, and the strain around his mouth communicated how angry he was on her behalf.

And maybe over whatever had upset him on the phone earlier, too. She mustn't forget he was already having a bad day.

His hand went to the small of her back, and he guided her out of the office onto the street. Before she could say anything to Thatcher, Sadie and Juniper turned the corner, coming toward them.

Bliss forced a smile. "Don't say anything, please, so I can tell Juniper myself tonight. Later, you and I can talk, if that's okay."

"More than okay."

After making small talk for a minute, they got into their respective vehicles and returned to Foxtail. The entire ride, Juniper chattered about all the fun she had with Sadie at The Bean Machine. Thatcher asked questions, but Bliss allowed the conversation to swirl around her. Maybe she was a terrible foster mom for not better engaging in the conversation, but she was so upset about losing her job, it was difficult to concentrate on anything else. She would have to tell Juniper the truth, but there was enough bitterness in life that Bliss would let Juniper enjoy today's sweetness.

Lord, I trust You to provide, but I ask that You show me what to do next.

Because she had to do *something*. Tonight, after Mick's party and after Juniper went to bed, Bliss would have to start looking for work. Surely, someone in town was looking for a full-time hire. She'd do anything, even though it meant she probably would no longer have the flexibility to work from home and she would have to find care for Juniper in the afternoons. A living wage was important, but benefits were more of a factor than salary. Once she adopted Juniper, she needed full health care. With Juniper's epilepsy—

"Almost there." Thatcher's comment tugged her from her musings. They were already turning into the ranch parking lot?

Bliss glanced at her watch. "Is it all right if Juniper and I hang out at your office until the party? It's about time for Coco's d-i-n-n-e-r." She spelled it so Coco wouldn't get too excited.

"No problem. You're more than welcome to come to my place if it's more comfortable, but I'm assuming you'll want to stay here where your car is parked."

"Thanks, but yeah, that was my thinking." Natalie's house—built after her marriage so she and her husband Wyatt could move out of the cramped family quarters where Thatcher lived and still resided on Foxtail property according to Asa's will—was within walking distance from the ranch office, just beyond the Granny Smith orchard at the farm, but she didn't want to have to walk back in the cold and dark after the party.

Not that she felt like attending a party after being fired. She would rather change into her pajamas and dig into the carton of Almond Mocha Fudge ice cream in the back of the freezer.

But she wanted to honor her friends. And the party might offer an opportunity to corner Thatcher before he did something silly like ask his cousins if Foxtail could hire her. They were kind people who would definitely take her on, but she couldn't—wouldn't—put her friends in a touchy position that they couldn't really afford.

Thatcher didn't bid them farewell at the door. "I need to pick up some things at my place, so I'll lock this up so it's set when you leave. Oh, and Juniper, the calves are getting bigger. Sometime after school, when it works for Bliss's schedule, let me know and we can take out the ATV to get a closer look."

"Yes!" Juniper practically squealed.

Bliss mouthed her thanks as he set the lock. He was so good to Juniper, and she adored their trips onto the ranch to see the babies…even though the calves weren't so little anymore.

Once Thatcher left, Bliss retrieved Coco's food and portable bowl from the pink bag. While Coco munched her kibble, Bliss and Juniper played a few rounds of Twenty Questions until it was time to hop in her black SUV for the short drive to Natalie and Wyatt's house.

"Are you excited to see the twins?" She glanced in the rearview mirror to catch Juniper's reaction. Wyatt and Natalie's adopted daughters were almost three years old, cute as proverbial buttons, and they adored Juniper.

The feeling was mutual. "Always, but Zoe will be there, too. Her dad and Dr. Mick are friends."

"Oh, that's right." Bliss thanked God for the smile on Juniper's face. All she wanted was a happy girl. A happy *daughter*. But now, the dream of adopting her was in jeopardy. Fear formed a painful lump in her throat.

They were met at the front door of Natalie's cabin-style home by one of the Foxtail orchard managers, Beatie Underhill. In her late sixties with long graying hair, she wore jeans and a red Foxtail sweatshirt. She propped the door open for them with her hip while stroking the mane of a miniature pinto horse.

"Hello, Gidget," Juniper greeted the Coco-sized, brown-and-white horse in a singsong voice. "And you, too, Mrs. Underhill."

Beatie laughed. "Hi, kiddo. Come on in."

Bliss hugged Beatie, patted the adorable little horse that offered Beatie stability now that the woman's macular degeneration caused vision and balance issues, and entered the two-story-high foyer. The house was warm, the air rich with the aroma of cooking food and the buzz of conversation among the guests.

Juniper didn't bother to take off her coat. "Zoe's in the living room, Bliss."

"Okay," she called after the girl as she hustled away.

"How's she doing?" Beatie's eyes narrowed while Bliss shrugged out of her coat.

"Great. No seizures in a month."

Beatie smiled. "Praise the Lord. That child has been through so much."

Far more than the epilepsy. Juniper's mom had sadly overdosed when Juniper was four, shortly after her father was incarcerated on multiple drug charges. Little Juniper had lived with Vera until the stroke two years ago, when she'd moved in with Bliss. Bliss's prayer was to provide Juniper stability, peace and more love than her young heart could hold.

But how could she do that if she didn't have a job?

The front door opened, and Thatcher strode in with a package of marshmallows and a large white bowl in his hands. He sniffed the air like she'd seen a bear do at a campsite once—on hind legs, nose high. "Hey, Beatie. Do I smell your garlic roasted potatoes?"

"Sure do." Beatie patted Thatcher's cheek, then peeked into the bowl he carried. "Is that your pasta salad, my boy?"

"Yup. Just need to add a few things before it's ready." He balanced the marshmallows atop the bowl and then pulled a plastic-wrapped ball of mozzarella from a jacket pocket.

"What are the marshmallows for?" Beatie frowned. "Those won't go with the salad."

"They're for Mick. Long story." He stepped back. "Gotta finish the salad."

"I need to go and…help him." Bliss offered Beatie a hasty smile and followed Thatcher.

It took her a few minutes to reach the kitchen, though, because she stopped to thank Wyatt and Natalie for hosting the party, wish Mick a happy birthday, exchange "Hey, long time no see" jokes with Sadie, add her card with a certificate for The Bean Machine inside of it to the other presents on the coffee table, greet Zoe's parents and Pastor Luke and wave at Beatie's husband, Dutch. All with as much haste as possible without seeming completely rude.

Thankfully, Thatcher was alone in the kitchen when she found him, cutting the mozzarella into cubes.

"We need to talk."

His glance told her he wasn't surprised. "Wanna make a lettuce salad while we do? Natalie got busy and asked if I could throw one together to go with the pasta one." He tipped his chin at a plastic container of spring mix on the counter, set beside a clear glass bowl and a cutting board laden with carrots, celery and a large red tomato.

"Sure." She washed up at the sink, scrubbing her hands with the lavender-scented soap. "I'll make this quick. You were so kind to offer to hire me, but you can't."

He slid the cheese from the cutting board into his salad. "Foxtail needs a bookkeeper. We had one when Asa made up his will, so it was permissible for us to hire you when Natalie needed more time with the girls. So, if we have to hire one now anyway, why shouldn't it be you?"

"As grateful as I am, Thatcher, it's not a full-time position. I need one of those, not just to live on, but so I can adopt Juniper."

Thatcher's brow furrowed. "I didn't think of that. I can't believe Gunther fired you like that. I have a few choice words for him."

She patted his clenched fist, hoping he'd relax. "I think he got the message already."

"Not the one I really wanted to give him, but now that I'm going to church, I'm watching my words. Still, I don't like seeing women—moms—treated poorly by their employers. My dad was never around when I was a kid and my mom went through a lot. I didn't like seeing you in that position, either."

No one had ever been this upset on her behalf before. She was so accustomed to bearing every burden herself, until she began handing them over to God. Well, attempting to give them to Him, anyway. She still had a habit of snatching her concerns back from God to worry about them.

But still, Thatcher's instinct to defend her felt nice, even if she was relieved that he hadn't given into it by growling at Gunther.

"I'm sorry your mom had a rough time, and I appreciate your support more than you know. But I'll be okay." Somehow. She dumped the spring mix into the glass bowl. "You, on the other hand? You're out a bookkeeper unless you go back to Gunther. There's no one else in town to do this sort of job."

"No way. The guy's a snake. We want you."

"I want to stay on with Foxtail, but...this conversation

is going around in circles." She started slicing the celery into neat little U's. "You're not usually like this, Thatcher."

"Like what?"

"Almost bossy." She smiled so he would understand she was teasing.

His lips twitched while he sprinkled oregano atop his salad. "Natalie says I have a tendency to try to fix people's problems when maybe all they want is to be listened to. I should've asked you what you needed before I yapped at you. So, I'm here to listen if you want to talk without any further advice." He stole a chunk of celery from her board and munched it.

"I appreciate that. And I'm here to listen to you, too, if you want to talk about what upset you earlier today."

"Are you shifting the topic from you to me, now?" He arched a single dark eyebrow.

She wished she had the ability to do that with her brows. "Maybe. I know myself, and it's easier to give help than to receive it. And I can't think of a single time you've asked me for anything."

He laughed. "Yeah, I guess I don't ask for help too often. And when I do, like today…"

"Yeah?" She cut a tomato in half, then quarters.

"It doesn't go how I expect it to."

"That sounds relatable." She slid tomato chunks into the bowl.

"Bliss?"

She had never heard this tone in his voice. When she looked up, his gaze tethered hers so she couldn't look away.

"You're a single woman trying to adopt a child, and as of today, you don't have a job. So when I say this, Bliss, it's only because I want to help."

He sounded so somber, dread pooled in her stomach. "Say what?"

"Maybe you need a husband."

A what now?

Thatcher's attempt to lighten the mood by making a goofy joke wasn't funny. He had no way of knowing how unhappy her marriage had been, though, so she tried to keep her tone light. "If you're trying to be humorous, stick to knock-knock jokes."

"I'm serious." His stare was so intense he didn't even blink. "Marriage could solve some of your problems immediately."

"And create a heap more." She'd already had a husband, and he'd left her with nothing. It was time to make it clear to Thatcher that this topic of conversation was officially closed. "I heard about Beatie and Dutch playing matchmaker with Sadie and Mick, but I didn't expect it from you, too. Now, I'm going to take this salad out to the dining room and we can forget this conversation ever happened." She gathered the glass bowl and turned away.

"What if it's me?"

She stopped. Rotated back to face him. "What did you say?"

He looked her straight in the eye, his cocoa-dark eyes soft. "You could marry me, Bliss."

The dish slipped from her hands and shattered at her feet.

Thatcher's first instinct was to check Bliss for an injury. Hands, ankles, lower legs. Anywhere broken glass might have bounced from the floor and cut her. "Are you okay?"

"I'm so sorry." Bliss's voice shook. "There's salad everywhere. And glass."

"I couldn't care less about those. Stand still and don't touch anything."

"You're being bossy again." Bliss bent to grab a shard of glass with her bare fingers.

"Sorry. I just don't want you getting hurt." He unlatched the child-safe locks on the cupboard beneath the sink and pulled out the trash can, dustpan and brush.

She dropped the large chunk into the trash can, and they must have both shifted to gather more debris at the same time because their heads collided with an audible smack.

"Too late," she joked with a wince. "Are you all right?"

Thatcher's crown pounded, but it would pass. "I've got a hard head. How are you?"

"Mortified." She flushed as red as the tomato that had splattered over her buff boots. "I owe Natalie a salad bowl."

"It's actually my bowl. I left it here last week." He handed her a towel and then started to brush up the wreckage into a pile. "I never liked it, anyway. Too foofy."

She took the dustpan and angled it so he could better scoop a chunk of veggies from the floor. "I appreciate you trying to make me feel better. About the bowl, I mean. Not the joke."

"I wasn't joking about getting married."

"But we're friends. Not—*that*," she sputtered.

Yikes. He hadn't meant to give that impression. "I'm suggesting a legal arrangement that's mutually beneficial. Nothing more."

Her pretty eyes narrowed. "I have a hard time believing you have a problem that would be alleviated by getting married, Thatcher. What's going on?"

His cousin's kitchen wasn't the ideal place for this discussion, but it couldn't wait. The answer to his plight was literally standing in front of him.

And he could be the answer to hers.

Thankfully, no one had come running when the bowl shattered. The party noise had covered the sound of breaking glass, so they were still alone. "I inadvertently triggered a proviso in Asa's will. If I don't marry, I lose the ranch."

Shock etched her pretty features. "That's preposterous."

"I know."

"Forcing marriage on someone isn't legal."

"True."

"Then why would Asa put this on you? He already forced you and your cousins to move to Foxtail, and if one of you fails, Foxtail gets sold and you all lose—oh, are there new requirements for them, too?"

"Nah, I'm special." In a lousy way. "Regardless of whether I fail or succeed from this point out, Natalie, Sadie and Dove will be okay as long as they follow the original will." He ducked beneath the sink to retrieve some spray cleaner. "That's what I did to cause this mess—I called the estate lawyer to ask if there were any loopholes that would allow me to move the north fence to include fresh pasture, or plant alfalfa."

"A totally sensible request."

"But one Asa anticipated I would make, and he must have known I would be the only one who would challenge his will, because he didn't set up any demands like this on my cousins."

It made Thatcher feel small, like his uncle thought little of him.

And he hated feeling like that. Bad enough he had no choice over where he lived or worked or how he ran his business. But it sure felt like Asa had set him up for a life of frustration from the start. First by hosting Thatcher every long, glorious summer of his growing up years, pouring his knowledge of cattle and the ranch into him as if he were grooming Thatcher to one day take over Foxtail Ranch.

But when Thatcher reached adulthood and expected to work the ranch, Asa claimed to not have room for him on the small staff. He told him he'd have a place for him when the time was right, whatever that meant.

Hurt, Thatcher took a job an hour's drive away at a larger ranch, where he'd gained skill and experience. He was close enough to visit his friends and family in Goldenrod, but Asa never had a place for him.

Until he died three years ago, that is.

Thatcher's love of Foxtail Ranch hadn't faded, but there were cracks of pain running through it. Nevertheless, he had willingly placed himself under the authority of his uncle's will for his cousins' sake. It was the only way to protect their inheritance as well as his.

And as complicated as things had been with his uncle, Thatcher did love Foxtail. Five years of submission to the unorthodox rules would be worth it in the end to call the ranch his own.

If only he'd kept his big mouth shut.

"So if you get married, you can keep the ranch."

"Not only that, but I'll be free to expand it. Knock down the fence, even plant alfalfa so I can provide for my own needs. I'd need a loan to make those improvements, but none of that will matter if I lose the ranch."

The hue of Bliss's large eyes had shifted from blue to gray, cloudless sky to storm. "I'm no legal analyst or anything, but can't you challenge this in court?"

"I could try, but Uncle Asa made it clear that if we contest the will, we automatically forfeit the inheritance." He swiped the last of the vegetable juices from the floor. "I did this to myself."

"No, you didn't. Asa did. And I completely understand why you reached out to the lawyer. You're running a ranch with one hand tied behind your back. If you want to get married, well, I understand that, too, but I doubt your girlfriend will be okay with you asking me out of pity because I lost my job today."

He grunted. "I don't have a girlfriend."

"Since when?"

"Since… I don't know. High school."

"But you always have one. *Thatcher Dalton, Ladies' Man.*" She spread her hand like she was reading the words off an imaginary banner.

Wow, his reputation hadn't caught up to the changes in his life. As much as he wanted to shrug off her observation, he owed her complete honesty. "It wasn't a big deal before I started going to church, but I haven't been on a date since I became a Christian. I didn't want anyone to develop expectations, since I never intended to get married."

Until now, when he realized that a single woman and friend, who stood directly in front of him, could benefit from such an arrangement, too.

She bit her lip. "I didn't mean to offend you."

"No, I get it." He opened a cupboard and found a wooden bowl for a fresh green salad. "I'm no knight in shining armor, but if you're my wife?" It felt weird to say the word. "I'll provide for you and Juniper so the adoption can progress as scheduled. I'd be able to keep my ranch, which is all I want."

She stared out the window, as if thinking.

"We'd have to live on Foxtail property, per the original will, but that will only last for two more years until the conditions are met, or whenever we decide to end our arrangement. The will says I only have to get married within six months. It didn't say for how long. Next year at this time, our lives could all be back to normal."

She opened the package of spring mix and dumped what was left of the contents into the wooden bowl. "No."

"To which part?"

"All of it. I have Juniper to consider."

"Precisely. The adoption can proceed as scheduled if you have my income."

"I'm worried about more than that. What about the rest of her life? Regardless of how businesslike our 'marriage' might be, she's a child. She would look at you as a father figure. That's no small thing, and if you walked out after six months? A year? I can't let her get hurt like that."

Oh.

He'd never thought he'd be a father. Or stepfather. So he'd never thought about letting a child down.

But a strong sense of protectiveness flowed through him, and his decision came quickly.

"Parenthood isn't easy, even if a person's had the best role models, which my dad and Uncle Asa…weren't. But I want to learn, and if you say yes, I trust God—and you—to guide me. I think the world of Juniper, and I promise to do my best for her, forever. I won't end the marriage, Bliss, but if you ever decide to? I promise I won't ditch Juniper. Ever."

Her mouth opened, then closed, like she was about to say no again. Rejection spread hot and thick through his gut.

It wasn't necessarily an appropriate reaction, though. It was only right that Juniper was Bliss's highest priority. And it wasn't like Bliss was rebuffing him romantically. He'd never thought of her that way.

Not because she wasn't likable or attractive. Even now, with a curtain of blond hair sweeping over her cheek, he resisted the urge to take it in his fingers and test if it was as silky as it looked—

Which was definitely not an acceptable action for a friend to take. Nor was it proper in the context of a rancher/bookkeeper dynamic.

Then again, neither was proposing marriage to her.

So it surprised him when she pushed the celery across the gray granite counter toward him, as if to encourage him to slice a new stalk. "I'll pray about it."

He felt like he could breathe again. "You will?"

"Yes. But I don't want us to speak about this to anyone until we come to a decision one way or another, okay? I don't want to confuse Juniper, or get her hopes up."

He grabbed a knife and started chopping. "Get her hopes up? You think she'd like us getting married?"

"She wants a family. A larger one than just the two of us." Bliss sliced a carrot into small coins. "And she thinks the world of you."

"The feeling is mutual, and the last thing I'd ever want to do is hurt that kid, so yeah, let's keep this between us. I'm not ready to tell my cousins about their dad's addendum, anyway."

They would only be upset—at their dad, and maybe at Thatcher for going to the lawyer without talking to them first. Until he knew how he would handle the situation, he would spare them from learning about yet another of Asa's controlling conditions. One that, if Thatcher followed it, would grant him allowances his cousins weren't entitled to make with their own enterprises.

Asa's addendum wasn't fair to any of them.

Bliss dropped the carrots atop the spring mix. "Am I the first woman to ever say no to you?"

He snorted. "For marriage, yeah. First one I ever asked, though."

"You didn't ask, technically." She rolled her eyes. "Go ahead and add the celery when you've finished. Too bad we're out of tomatoes now, though. This salad won't be as good as the last, but hopefully no one notices because your pasta salad looks so good. I want the recipe."

He tossed celery atop the carrots. "If we get married, you won't need it. I'll make it for you whenever you want."

"Oh, um. Right." She pressed her lips together.

They carried the bowls to the dining room and set them among other the dishes for Mick's birthday feast—apple-cider baked beans laced with bacon, Dove's yeast rolls, chicken tenders for the kids, a fruit salad and Beatie's garlic roasted potatoes, chock-full of fragrant, golden-brown cloves that made his mouth water.

"I'll catch you later." Bliss slipped into the living room, where everyone else had gathered.

Wyatt passed her on his way into the dining room. "I was just looking for you, Thatcher. I want your take on the tri-tip before I pull it off the grill."

"Sure." Thatcher followed him outside to the patio. It was too dark to take in the mountain scenery, but from out here he had a clear view of what was happening on the other side of the wide living room windows. Bliss was chatting with Zoe's parents, appearing far more serene than he felt after their discussion. Behind her, Mick, the man of the hour, had an arm around Sadie, whispering something in her ear that made her laugh.

Wyatt followed Thatcher's gaze and chuckled. "I hope I was never that bad when Natalie and I were engaged."

"The first engagement or the second?" Thatcher couldn't resist ribbing his friend. "But yeah, you were."

Wyatt removed the lid to the grill and they were surrounded by the delicious aroma of spice-rubbed beef. "That's love, I guess."

Not that Thatcher knew personally. Thatcher had decided a long time ago that it was better to stay single, rather than end up like his role models—his dad, Jake, and Jake's older brother, Asa, had both made disasters of their marriages. It hadn't been a difficult choice for Thatcher to live with. He'd met many women he liked. But loved?

It wasn't in his DNA, if his dad and uncle were anything to judge by. Marriage wouldn't change that. But fatherhood? Well, stepfatherhood, if that was a word. He would need God's wisdom and strength if he were going to give Juniper all she needed.

Feeling a bit more at peace about his future prospects, he gave the roast on the grill a good once-over. "Perfect." He transferred it to a platter, dodging Wyatt's dog, Ranger, on his way back inside the house, but his thoughts fixed on the prospect of parenting Bliss's foster daughter.

Maybe he should have prayed before proposing to Bliss, but he'd start asking for God's wisdom and direction now. He cared about Bliss and Juniper.

He wouldn't expect them to *want* someone like him forever, but he'd be present for them as long as they *needed* him.

With God's help, he wouldn't be like his dad or uncle. Not when it came to parenthood. He would break the cycle and be a man who kept his promises.

Chapter Three

February arrived with a hard frost that showed no sign of thawing, its grip as unyielding as the muscle tension in Bliss's neck and shoulders as she searched for work. By Wednesday, five days after Mick's party, she had exhausted all job leads, and she had no idea what to do about Thatcher's unorthodox proposal.

She didn't discuss it with her closest friend, Olivia, or anyone in their knit and crochet group. Thatcher's reason was too personal to broadcast, so she chose instead to figure it out by herself. With God's help, of course, but her prayers had not been answered by an electronic billboard flashing yes or no, as much as she wished it were that easy to discern His will.

However, a few things nudged at her, like Juniper and Coco's excitement at seeing Thatcher at church on Sunday. The way he jumped in to help set up tables in the parish hall for a special luncheon. And Juniper peppering her about Thatcher after school every day. *When can we go out on the ATV to see the calves?* And, *Can you ask Thatcher for his pasta salad recipe?*

Bliss had to smile at that, recalling how Thatcher had said if she married him, she wouldn't need her own copy because he would prepare it for her.

Her late husband, Lane, hadn't cooked. Nor would he have swept up shards of broken glass the way Thatcher had, either. Something about Thatcher's first instinct being Bliss's safety, while saying nothing of the mess or waste of the bowl or salad ingredients, soothed a frayed corner of her heart.

Perhaps that was why she'd agreed to meet Thatcher today at the ranch office for the short walk to a little Craftsman-style house surrounded by pines and scrub oaks, where he thought they could live if they married.

"The ranch's former owner lived here before Asa bought the property," Thatcher explained as he opened the creaky wooden door. "Since then, it's been used for storage."

The living room was half-full of old metal file cabinets and stacks of cardboard banker's boxes. Sweeping her gaze over the space, Bliss tried to look past the dust-covered items. The place had good bones, and her nose didn't detect must or mold.

"I hate to uproot you and Juniper." He ruffled the hair at the back of his head, leaving it disheveled but also somehow incredibly appealing. "But if we have to live on Foxtail property, this is the best option. My little apartment in the farmhouse is too small for the three of us. Well, four, with Coco."

"I've seen Dove's apartment, and if yours is the same size, then you're right." One bedroom and a postage-stamp-sized living area.

"I've put some money aside for a rainy day, so I can fix this place up—new appliances, paint, whatever you want. I thought I could put in a screen door to let in the evening breeze, and there's room for a porch swing. That oak out front has the perfect branch for a swing for Juniper. She's the reason I want to move quickly on this. Her adoption process, I mean. This place will take a few weeks to fix up, but I thought we could live in the rental cabin behind the farmstand until then."

Bliss and Juniper had attended the Foxtail staff Christmas party at the rental cabin not even two months ago. While she and Juniper had spent most of the crisp evening out at the firepit, enjoying s'mores and carols, they'd eaten their dinner inside. She recalled that it was well-appointed and boasted three bedrooms, one for each of them.

As Foxtail's bookkeeper, she knew the cabin wasn't rented out much in the winter months, so living there wouldn't cost Foxtail valuable bookings. "Sounds perfect, if your cousins are okay with us living there."

"I'm sure they will be, once we explain what's going on."

She caught her lower lip between her teeth. "The night of Mick's party, you said you wouldn't dissolve the marriage. I want to make clear that you aren't expecting me to do it eventually, because divorce isn't an option for me."

Even though she had been in the divorce process when Lane died. It hadn't been her choice, though.

Thatcher just shrugged. "I'm signing up for a lifetime commitment."

"But what if you meet someone else? Someone you actually love?"

"I won't."

His emphatic response drew her up short. "You can't know that. You have a lot of life left, Thatcher."

"So do you."

"My priority is Juniper. I'm not interested in a relationship."

"Me neither. That forever love thing isn't real, not for me. For other people, sure."

Odd words from a man who used to date all the time,

but he had told her that he wasn't that guy anymore. Not since starting to attend church.

What if he went back to his old ways? What if he changed his mind and left her—

Bliss slammed the door on that pesky thought. Thatcher was not Lane. He had given his life to God, he had promised to be around for Juniper forever, and he was a good man who cared about his family.

And this marriage would never touch her heart the way her first one had. Therefore, it couldn't destroy her.

She realized Thatcher had started pacing, reminding her of how he'd behaved when he talked on the phone with the estate lawyer. What agitated him so much?

Maybe he had a lot of work waiting for him. She recalled something about turning the bulls out, so she wouldn't keep him. "I'd like to look at the bedrooms and bathroom, but if you need to get back to the ranch, go ahead."

"I left Frank in charge." His foreman. "He and the hands have everything covered."

If he wasn't feeling rushed to return to work, then what was stressing him out so much?

Surely not her response to the house?

She hadn't answered his question yet, though, had she?

"This house is in better shape than my grandpa's, but my grandpa's house is bigger and I'm quite partial to it." The pretty but dilapidated gingerbread-style house was next door, although there was an acre of land between their houses—his side was grazing land, and hers was the dying pear orchard. "Would you be willing to move there when Asa's will is satisfied?"

"I'll do anything to make this work."

"Then, I think this little house will be fine for the next two years."

His stopped pacing and his full lips twitched. "Does that mean you'll marry me?"

It sure sounded like it, didn't it?

She gulped. "Maybe?"

"Then since you're still deciding, could we pray about it together? Now?"

It seemed so intimate a thing to do, and yet prayer was the very foundation she wanted for her family. Feeling almost shy, she nodded.

Thatcher didn't take her hands, just stood in front of her. When he closed his eyes, she did the same.

"Lord, thank You for caring for us in our times of heartache, even when those times are of our own making. In my case, anyway. We seek Your will, and I ask that whatever is best for Bliss and Juniper, You would show it to them. And if that's with me, Lord, we ask Your blessing. Forgive me for not seeking You first thing, and help me come to You instead of trying to fix everything myself. We wait on You, Lord. In Jesus's name, amen."

"Amen," Bliss echoed.

His smile warmed her to her toes and touched something in her heart. The future wouldn't be without its ups and downs, but she felt more confident facing it with a praying partner who went to the Lord with her.

Then she knew her answer.

But she couldn't commit to it. Not yet. "I'll talk to Juniper this afternoon, and if she's okay with it, then…yes."

His eyes darkened like melted chocolate. "All right, then. I'll start repairs by fixing the heater." He rapped his knuckles on the wall by the thermostat. "Maybe we should look at appliances together so we're sure to get what you like."

She bit back a laugh. Only a bride who was marrying for

convenience would be perfectly fine with her brand-new fiancé's first words to her having to do with home repairs.

But in truth, she was more than fine with it. The idea of picking out a stove and a refrigerator made her almost giddy. "That would be fabulous. We need to clean this place out, too. Is there a place to move these?" She almost patted one of the boxes but remembered the dust in time to spare herself a dirty hand.

"The storage barn, where we keep Foxtail's holiday decorations, I guess. I should probably go through them first. Some of the paperwork might be so outdated that I can shred it."

"Since I'm unemployed, I can do it. If I find personal files, I'll set them aside."

"That would be great, thanks."

Bliss glanced at her watch. Two o'clock. "I have to pick up Juniper from school. I'll text you later, okay?"

"Sounds good." He followed her out and locked up the house behind him.

She prayed the entire way to the elementary school, and she was still praying when she pulled her black SUV to the front of the pickup line where Juniper was playing a clapping game with Zoe. Coco lounged contentedly on the grass at Juniper's feet.

Bliss hit the button to roll down the passenger-side window. "Hi, girls. Do you need a ride home, Zoe?"

"No, thanks. My grandma is on her way." Zoe ran to the door. "But we wanted to ask you if Juniper can come over this weekend."

"Sounds fun. I'll text your mom, okay?"

Zoe nodded. "Bye, Mrs. Anderson. Bye, Juniper. Bye, Coco-Puff."

Bliss turned away so the girls wouldn't see the emotion

in her eyes. This was what she wanted for Juniper, a best friend and as carefree a childhood as possible, despite the difficulties she faced as a young person with epilepsy. Juniper had been through so much with drug-addicted parents, and then Vera's stroke. The only reason she was willing to marry Thatcher was Juniper's welfare.

A rush of nerves skittered through her belly as Juniper climbed into the backseat. *Lord, grant me wisdom as I ease into this discussion.* "Want to go to the craft store? I thought we could see if they have any new latch-hook kits. Then maybe we can grab an ice cream."

Juniper adored latch hook. Her bed was already piled high with pillows she had fashioned from kits—a sloth, a snowman and butterflies, but she was always up to making more. "Yes. Coco says so, too."

"I'm glad you two are in agreement." Bliss engaged her turn signal and headed farther east into town. "Did you and Coco have a good day at school?"

"I aced my spelling test," Juniper announced. "Coco wanted a chicken nugget that fell on the cafeteria floor at lunchtime, but she didn't go for it because she was working. And I didn't want her to eat it because the floor is yucky, anyway."

"We'll give her a treat at home." Bliss had just stocked up on a few of Coco's favorite varieties from the pet store.

They spent a pleasant twenty minutes browsing the latch-hook kits before Juniper selected a box with an image of a cute cartoon fox. Mindful of her need to pinch pennies, Bliss didn't buy yarn for her own crochet projects, which was probably best since she had dozens of unopened skeins at home. The name of her knit and crochet group, Knit Addicts, was apt for her.

Next, they strode two doors down to The Creamery, ordered at the 1950s-style soda counter, then gravitated toward a red booth in the corner.

During the summer and harvesttime, The Creamery was always full of tourists who visited Goldenrod to hike, camp or, in September and October, pick apples from Foxtail Farm or one of the other orchards in the vicinity. On a Wednesday in early February, however, Bliss and Juniper were the only customers.

Bliss retrieved Coco's portable water bottle from her bag and offered the sweet pup a drink while she and Juniper tucked into dishes of cookie dough chocolate swirl with hot fudge and peanuts on top.

"I don't care that the weather is too cold for ice cream." Juniper grinned, unaware of the chocolate smudging her mouth. "This tastes so good."

"It does." Bliss tugged two paper napkins from the metal dispenser atop the table. "Do you mind if we have a little talk while we eat?"

"Is it about the adoption?"

No. But yes, at its core.

She might as well cut to the chase. "It's about, well, Thatcher. He asked me to marry him." The words sounded surreal, but she plowed ahead. "I told him I wanted to discuss it with you first—"

Juniper dropped her spoon into the glass dish and, squealing, slipped from her seat to come to Bliss's side of the booth for a hug. "You said yes, didn't you?"

"I didn't tell him one way or another." Bliss held her close, relishing the moment. "I wanted to know what you thought."

"I think you should say yes, but isn't it more important what *you* think?"

Something damp and hot nuzzled Bliss's hand, so she

opened the embrace to include Coco, who eagerly wedged herself between them. "Nope. You, Coco and I are a team."

"Well, Coco likes Mr. Thatcher. And so do I." Juniper slipped out of Bliss's hold and rubbed Coco beneath her chin. "He's big and funny and nice. Will he adopt me?"

"I don't know. But he loves hanging out with you."

"He likes hanging out with you, too. I knew he loved you. I just knew it."

Oh dear. She didn't want to tell Juniper that Thatcher most assuredly did not love her, but she didn't want to explain a marriage of convenience to a nine-year-old, either. "What makes you say that?"

Juniper settled back in her chair. "He's always smiling and whistling when you're around him."

"He's a happy guy." Bliss swirled her spoon through her hot fudge.

"He's happier with you. Except for the day you lost your job. I think he wanted to yell at Mr. Berg. But what I want to know is why you kept your *courtship* a secret from me." Juniper enunciated the word she had learned from Bliss reading *Little Women* to her at bedtime. "You never went on any dates, did you? Or did you just decide to skip all that gooshy stuff?"

"Something like that." Bliss took a sip of ice water.

"I don't blame you. That stuff is gross." Juniper stuck out her tongue. "But I say you should marry him. I've wanted a real family forever, and now I'm getting one."

"We're already a real family, Juniper. It's just not official until the adoption hearing."

"I know, but I want a dad and aunts and uncles and a little sister or brother, too. It was my Easter wish last year."

This was news. "Easter wish?"

"Like a birthday wish, but on Easter." Juniper swallowed

a bite of her sundae. “My mom and I used to do it, because she said spring was a time of new beginnings. I don’t think wishes really come true, but they’re fun to make, anyway. Is that bad?”

“No, honey.” But this particular wish would never come all the way true. Bliss and Thatcher would not have a lovey-dovey marriage, and there would be no little siblings. Bliss couldn’t tell Juniper that, of course, but what could she share that was appropriate to her young age?

“I’m sorry there won’t be siblings, honey. But I can’t. Well, I never could when I was married.”

She’d tried. Countless times. Endured tests and grief and the shame Lane and his family, and hers, heaped on her.

Juniper stared at her for a second. “Is that why you fostered me? Because you wanted to be a mom but couldn’t?”

“I wanted to be a mom, but no, that is not why.” Bliss covered Juniper’s hand with hers. “I wanted you because of *you.* You’re such an amazing person, I couldn’t imagine living without you. And that’s the truth.”

A faint smile played on Juniper’s lips. “Okay.”

“Okay.” Bliss loved her so much it was hard not to cry.

Juniper spooned the last bit of her ice cream into her mouth. “When is the wedding?”

“I don’t know.” Within six months, though.

“Can I text Grandma and tell her?”

“I’d better tell Thatcher first that we say yes, seeing as he’s the groom and all.” Bliss winked. But inside she was quaking. Not out of fear or whatever the matrimonial version of buyer’s remorse was. But with excitement, because now she didn’t need to race to find a full-time job or move out of town for work. She would be able to adopt Juniper on schedule.

That night, after finishing the dinner dishes, Bliss typed out a text to Thatcher.

It's a go. Juniper and I accept.

She added a diamond ring emoji to drive it home for Thatcher.

He must have had his phone right beside him, because he immediately sent back a series of exclamation points. Then another bubble appeared.

Wow, two lovely ladies. Three, if you count Coco. Am I blessed or what?

She responded with a laughing face, then tapped out more.

I'm grateful.

She waited while he typed, watching the series of three dots on the screen until his message appeared.

When?

It seemed easier to find a date that worked for her than him. With her limited understanding of ranch work, she had no clue what his weekends looked like. He wasn't as busy now as he had been during fall calving, but...she was clueless.

My schedule is wide open. How about yours?

There was a pause, and then a longer text appeared.

I don't want the adoption to be held up a minute longer than necessary. So if you don't mind a small courthouse-style wedding, how about next Saturday? I just did a search online and found a place that issues licenses and officiates service, same-day service. They have openings next Saturday.

Just over a week away? Her heart skittered. That was sooner than she'd expected, but…there was no reason to wait, was there?

She sent a thumbs-up emoji. He responded with another text.

How about I invite my family to the farmhouse for brunch after church Sunday so we can tell them together? Nothing fancy. I'll make breakfast burritos. Anyone you want to invite?

As much as she liked his family, they were a tight-knit group, and she preferred to tell her friends like Olivia—and her family—at her own pace.

Not that her parents would care much. They hadn't even bothered to meet Juniper.

No thanks. But tell me what to bring for the burritos.

Juniper was going to love living with him for the food alone.

They texted a little more before she set down her phone.

She was engaged. Something she had doubted would ever happen again.

This was nothing like her first engagement. No flowers, no diamonds, no professional photographer appearing at just the right time.

Not even the fiancé on bended knee.

But this engagement, this marriage, wasn't about romance. This was about adopting Juniper, for Bliss, and keeping the ranch, for Thatcher.

They were both getting what they wanted, and she didn't want to think ahead any further than that.

After church on Sunday, Thatcher whisked a dozen eggs with a fork and then poured them atop crumbled chorizo sausage in the frying pan. With a long, soft sizzle, the tantalizing aromas of eggs and spiced meat mingled with the scent of frying potatoes in a separate skillet.

"This is going to be delicious." Bliss, clad in a fuzzy gray sweater dress that matched the February sky outside, set out plates and paper napkins atop the table positioned where his apartment's living room and kitchen met. "Where do you keep the silverware?"

"Drawer to the right of the sink." He prodded the egg mixture with a spatula, keenly aware of her proximity behind him in this tiny space. "Be warned, it's sticky."

The drawer scraped as she tugged, accompanied by the racket of clattering utensils.

"You weren't kidding." Bliss's smile shone through her voice. "Let's see, seven forks and one, two…five spoons for the toppings—"

Her hip hit his leg. Not hard, only for a fraction of a second, but he jumped out of her way. "Sorry, I'm such a big oaf—"

"My fault."

"This kitchen is too small for two people once you open a drawer," he tried to joke, but the truth was, the kitchen was snug. He was glad they would live somewhere roomier.

But he was also keenly aware of her in this cramped space. Her floral perfume, the freckles dusting her nose and the way she took short, quick breaths, a sign she was nervous.

He was, too, but they shouldn't be nervous about being around each other.

"Bliss? If we're getting married?" He moved the egg mixture around the pan. "We have to get used to being in close quarters. It's awkward and weird, but we're bound to literally bump into each other once in a while. And it's okay, because we're friends."

"You're right." She shifted sideways and shoved the drawer shut. "Now all we have to be nervous about is getting through the next hour."

"Thankfully, my family doesn't bite. But they might not like hearing about Asa's addendum." And he didn't relish telling them about it.

"Hopefully, they will be in a good mood after a brunch of breakfast burritos."

Before she finished her sentence, his phone vibrated against the Formica countertop. *Doreen Dalton* scrolled over his screen. "It's my mom, finally returning my call. She's on FaceTime, if you want to say hi."

Bliss licked her lips in a gesture that told him she was still nervous. "Sure, just let me text Zoe's mom and check on Juniper first. Oh, and do you have salsa?"

"Three kinds, from hot to scorching. Fridge door." He shut off the stove and stepped around the short wall dividing the kitchen from the living room. Accepting his mom's call, he dropped onto the overstuffed charcoal-gray couch that had seen better days. "Hey, Mom."

"Hello, pumpkin. My, what a handsome shirt."

The button-down was the same hue as his couch, good for church but a long way from fancy, which Thatcher didn't do if he could help it. "Didn't you buy it for me?"

"Yes." Her laughter was rich and hearty. "Why are you dressed up? Do you have a date?"

He would never go on a date again, would he? The idea didn't bother him. "It's Sunday, Mom. I went to church."

"Oh, that's right. Well, I couldn't have gone if I had wanted to. It's a winter wonderland here, but what do you expect of Denver at this time of year?" She swung the phone camera around in a dizzying arc so she could show him the scene outside her window. Before he could make out much detail in the white blur, however, she swiveled the phone back so her round face was back on camera. With her short stature, blue eyes and wispy blond hair, she looked nothing like Thatcher, but he figured the genes on his dad's side must have overpowered hers. Everyone said he looked like Uncle Asa.

Her eyes curved into crescents as she smiled. "Happily, I won't be in this snow for long."

"That's right. You and Aunt Janet are off to Rome in a few days. How long is the cruise, again?"

"A full month, and then we've added on a few days at the tail end to sightsee. Isn't it silly that you sail in and out of Rome but they don't schedule any time to see the sites there? Thankfully, I'm in no rush to return home. I love being retired so far." She giggled like a kid.

"You deserve to have fun, Mom." After Jake had ditched his family for the road, music and motorcycles, his mother had worked tirelessly to provide for Thatcher in Los Angeles. Once Thatcher grew up and hired on at a ranch, she accepted a job transfer to Colorado, where she'd grown up. He loved that she was happy, but of course he also wished he could send her on a hundred cruises, if that was what she wanted. "Are you ready for the trip?"

"I'm all set—passport, good walking shoes and sunscreen. I even went to the doctor to refill my prescriptions, so I'll have everything I need while I'm gone. Oh, that reminds me, when I was leaving the doctor, there was one of those bloodmobiles in the parking lot. Guess what I did?"

He loved his mom's wide grin. "You didn't."

"I did. Your Gallon Club membership inspired me, so I pretended I'm not afraid of needles, and I donated."

"That's great, Mom. I'm proud of you for helping your community like that."

"It wasn't as bad as I thought it would be, and everyone was so nice. They said I'm a universal donor and told me how valuable that is, and to come back." She gestured at him. "All right, your turn."

His lips twitched. "To donate blood?"

"No, silly, to tell me what you're up to," his mom continued, her face so close to the camera that her nose took up most of his viewing screen.

He couldn't help but draw things out to tease her. "I washed the truck yesterday."

"Ho hum."

"I'm thinking of getting a new pair of work boots."

"What a thrilling life you lead."

"Oh, and I'm getting married."

Her squeal reminded him of a cartoon mouse's. "Thatcher Jacob Dalton, did you say what I think you said?"

"Yes, but it's what you would call an arrangement born of necessity, thanks to Uncle Asa."

"Asa?" Mom's smile flatlined. "Start from the beginning."

He did, and it wasn't clear if his mom approved or not, but she was gracious when Bliss came alongside him to tell his mother hello. They had met during his mom's last visit to California, but back then Bliss had been the bookkeeper, not the future daughter-in-law.

"If you two are sure about this, and you're both committed to little Juniper?" Mom's smile was small, but genuine. "Then, congratulations are in order. When's the wedding?"

"Saturday. Valentine's Day, as it happens."

Her small, round eyes widened. "So soon?"

"The three of us—Thatcher, Juniper and I—spoke to Juniper's case manager about dates, and this is the best solution, so we don't hold up the adoption process." Bliss sounded genuinely fearful she was causing offense, but that was Bliss. Conscientious to a *T.* "I'm so sorry you'll have to miss the ceremony, though."

His mom flapped her hand. "No worries, honey. I eloped myself. But I'd like to celebrate with you when I get back. I'm gonna be a sort-of-grandma, after all."

After a few more minutes of chat, Thatcher disconnected the call and let out a loud sigh of relief. "That went pretty well. Are you sure you don't want to call your mom and dad together?"

Bliss rose from the couch. "Not until after we're married. They wouldn't understand. I'm not sure my friends will, either, but I'll tell Olivia and the Knit Addicts tomorrow—privately, Olivia will get the unvarnished truth, but I'm not going to tell the others all the gory details."

Curiosity nagged at him, but he could hear Dove's footsteps in the hall outside his door as she made the short journey from her apartment to his. "Ready for round two?"

"Hopefully it goes as well as the talk with your mom did."

Her tremulous smile drew his attention to the sheen of her glossy lips, where his gaze lingered a moment too long.

Something shifted inside of him, like an awareness of her, not as a friend, but as a woman.

Duh, dude. Of course she's female. Now knock it off.

Lecturing himself to curb any future thoughts about Bliss's loveliness, he opened the door to admit Dove. She didn't attend church with the rest of the family, but she'd dressed up for brunch, donning a green turtleneck and pinning her dark hair atop her head. An excellent baker, she carried one of her award-winning apple pies, which was always a welcome sight.

"Hey Bliss, I didn't expect to see you here." Dove's bright tone sounded innocent enough, but her gaze darted between him and Bliss as if she were trying to figure out why their friend and bookkeeper was included in Thatcher's "family" brunch. "Is Juniper here, too?"

Bliss's cheeks turned a becoming shade of pink. "She's having lunch with Zoe's family."

"Hey, everyone." Sadie and Mick appeared behind Dove, holding hands. Like Dove, they eyed Bliss with happy surprise. Within about thirty seconds, Natalie and Wyatt arrived without their twin toddlers, Rose and Luna, who had gone to lunch with Wyatt's parents.

Thatcher knew they all had questions, but the food was getting cold. "Come on in. Everything is hot and ready in the kitchen. Eggs and chorizo, potatoes and fresh tortillas. You got the salsa, Bliss?"

She nodded. "Cheese and guacamole, too. Oh, and there's cantaloupe."

"Did you two cook together?" Natalie, who was just three months older than Thatcher, wasn't the sort to beat around the bush.

"Natalie, let them talk when they're ready," Sadie said out of the side of her mouth.

"Sorry, but when you invited us for a family brunch *without* the kids, Thatcher, we figured you had something to tell us. And Bliss being here—happy as I always am to see you, Bliss—well, my mind is racing."

Thatcher looked at Bliss. They had wanted to wait until everyone's stomachs were full, but the opportunity seemed to have fallen into his lap.

"I do have something to tell you." *Here goes.* "Bliss and I are getting married."

No one smiled. Or even blinked, until Sadie rushed toward him for a hug. "What a surprise."

"I didn't know you were dating," Wyatt mused.

"We aren't, actually." Bliss's interjection surprised Thatcher, but he was glad she'd brought it up.

He gestured toward the kitchen. "Why don't we dish up our food before it gets cold, and I'll explain."

Although his family members and their significant others crafted plump burritos, no one ate much while they sat in the cozy living room, listening to Thatcher's story about the addendum to Asa's will, Bliss's job loss and Juniper's adoption.

And his request to stay in the rental cabin for a few weeks while they fixed up the old house on the ranch.

Natalie, Dove and Sadie, seated side by side on the couch, listened intently, wearing matching expressions of shock. But when he finished, words tumbled out of their mouths so fast it was impossible to tell who said what.

"Why would Dad make you get married?"

"Why didn't he allow us the ability to make changes to our inheritances, too?"

"Was this designed to kick you out of Foxtail, Thatcher, or ensure you stayed in?"

All excellent questions that he had no answers to.

He felt Wyatt's hard stare before he met it. Wyatt's head tipped back toward the door. "Can we go outside for a sec?"

Thatcher didn't want Bliss to feel abandoned. "Is that okay with you?"

"We're not going to eat her, Thatcher. She's our friend." Dove sounded offended.

"It's fine." Bliss nodded.

Thatcher followed Wyatt and Mick out of his apartment, through the farmhouse's foyer onto the porch. The cold air felt good on his heated cheeks, and he prayed for an extra dose of patience as he dealt with his two closest friends, and now his family members—or in Mick's case, about to be.

He gripped the porch railing with both hands. "I know this is weird—"

"Do you remember when I came back to town after Rose and Luna were orphaned?" Wyatt folded his arms. "You pulled me onto this porch and warned me not to hurt Natalie. Well, the boot is on the other foot now. I don't want you hurting Bliss."

"I said that because you left Natalie, Wyatt." Thatcher stared up at the sky, shaking his head. "I'm not leaving Bliss, either. I'm marrying her."

"To hold on to your ranch." Wyatt held up his hand. "I know there's more to it than that, but Bliss doesn't deserve to get dumped once she's helped you."

Ouch. "What makes you think I would do that?"

"You do, man." Mick's voice was compassionate, despite the harshness of his words. "We care about you, but you've left a trail of broken hearts in your wake."

"You've never committed to anyone," Wyatt added.

"Good thing, or I wouldn't be free to help Bliss now. Look, she and I are friends, and that won't change."

"It could. Sadie was my best friend," Mick said, "and fake dating evolved into a real relationship."

"We aren't pretending anything, though, Mick. We're actually getting married. Moving into the same house, raising Juniper—"

"I'm glad you brought her up," Wyatt interrupted, "because it's one thing to hurt Bliss. It's another thing to confuse or upset that little girl. You can't abandon her if you get bored with Bliss, the way you have with every other woman you dated."

Thatcher clung to his temper by a thread. "I don't get bored. That's not why I never got serious, but—that's not important right now. I'm *not* going to ditch Juniper or Bliss. You might think I'm incapable of commitment, but I am determined to devote myself to this family, to my ranch, to raising Juniper and to my promises to Bliss. I told her I will never dissolve the marriage, and I don't take that lightly."

Mick sighed. "But Thatcher—"

"Bliss and I have a platonic, legal arrangement that will be mutually beneficial. Her eyes are wide open and so are mine. I'm sorry if you can't support us, but I hope you'll at least wish us well. Good thing we're keeping the ceremony private. Just us."

He left them there on the porch, marching back into his apartment. "Bliss, are you okay?"

"I'm fine, but it's about time for me to pick up Juniper."

"I'll walk you to your car." Maybe his family would get the hint and go to their respective homes. Dove and Sadie might share walls with him, but he could use a little space.

After she told his cousins goodbye and grabbed her purse and jacket, he linked arms with her and escorted her past the guys on the porch, around to the back of the house where the family parked their cars. He opened the door to Bliss's SUV and then leaned against the open frame.

She looked at him, wincing. "I'm sorry they don't approve. Is it me?"

"It's me." He rubbed his temple. "They think I'll hurt you."

"Because you don't love me?" Her gaze shifted past him. "They don't understand why we're doing this then. It's about love, but not *that* kind. I'm perfectly fine not having that sort of love again."

She had never spoken of her marriage to him before. "Losing your husband must have been awful."

"Lane was divorcing me." Her tone was flat. "He died in a snorkeling accident in Hawaii while in the company of another woman who was younger than me and could—well, it doesn't matter."

"It does to me."

"Could have a baby. Which I couldn't." She glanced at him. "Instead, I had cysts, a blockage and two miscarriages. A lot of hope followed by grief."

"Miscarriages?" *Oh, Bliss.*

"You said you didn't care about having kids of your own. If you did, I wouldn't have agreed to marry you because I'm not sure I could ever be able to. It wouldn't have been fair to you."

"That's not it at all, Bliss." Protectiveness roared through him like fire in his veins. "If I'd been around back then? I'd have wanted to rip Lane apart. But I'm here now, and it's going to take a lot of prayer to help me not hate that guy's guts." He grimaced. "I shouldn't talk like that, I know, but what kind of jerk weasels off with someone else?"

"He had left me, in an emotional sense, long before that." Her smile was thin. "But that has nothing to do with you and me, right here and now. So, since we have a wedding scheduled in six days, we have a decision to make. Do you still want to go through with it, even though your family isn't on board?"

"I do. Do you?"

She nodded. "I just wish it wasn't causing a wedge between you and your family."

"I love them, but this isn't about them."

She tapped a thumb on the steering wheel. Thatcher's gaze followed her hand—the blue veins protruding on the back, the ringless, slender fingers fidgeting on the vinyl. And then he knew what he wanted.

No regrets.

"Are you free for lunch tomorrow?"

"I'm free all day since Gunther let me go." She rolled her eyes. "What's up?"

"It's a surprise."

One he hoped she would like. But it was a necessary step if they were going to do this wedding thing right.

Chapter Four

Monday at Trixi's Diner downtown, Bliss swiped a chunk of sourdough around her bowl, sopping up the last of her tomato bisque.

Thatcher pushed away his empty burger plate. "Good soup?"

"Some people crave sugar, others salty snacks. But my downfall is cream. Not a single drop should be wasted." She popped the bread into her mouth, savoring the rich emulsion of tomato, basil and cream.

"Doughnuts are my weakness." He patted his flat stomach. "Dove's cider doughnuts are magnificent. Have you had one?"

"They're fantastic, but aren't they only available in the autumn?"

"Unfortunately." His grumble was completely contrived and exaggerated. "But the chain shop by the highway does the job."

"Now I know what to get you for your birthday. A gift card for doughnuts." Her cheeks hurt from smiling so much. Thatcher was funny and lighthearted, and it was good to hang out without talking about the stressors that had driven them to get married, although Thatcher did fill her in on the good talk he'd had with the loan officer at the bank the other day.

The future looked bright to expand the ranch…and for their family to be a happy—if unusual—one. "Thank you. I'm glad you suggested we grab lunch."

"It was fun." He grabbed the check. "Now for part two of our adventure."

"There's more?" She scooched out of the booth.

"I promised you a surprise, remember?"

"I assumed the location of our lunch was the surprise." And Trixi's Diner was always a good choice, as far as Bliss was concerned. Delicious food, friendly staff—

"Hiya, Thatcher. Long time no see." The female at the register used a tone that was indeed rather friendly, perhaps too friendly, in Bliss's opinion.

"Hi, Tammy." He sounded polite as he pulled bills out of his wallet. "Do you know Bliss?"

Bliss said hello while Tammy measured the gap between Bliss and Thatcher with her eyes, as if she was trying to decide whether she and Thatcher were more than friends.

The town gossips would have something to talk about when they heard about the wedding, wouldn't they? Little did they know that eligible bachelor Thatcher was only marrying her to keep his ranch. Bliss almost burst out laughing at the sheer ridiculousness of it all.

"What's so funny?" Thatcher's full lips twitched as he opened the diner door for her.

A cold, gentle breeze lapped over her cheeks. "Just thinking about how shocking our relationship will be to some people. We'll be the talk of the town."

"I don't care what anyone thinks. Or says. None of their business."

She liked how things rolled off Thatcher like water off

a duck. She strove to live more that way, too, but it was a hard habit to break. Growing up and even into her marriage, she had found that life went a lot more smoothly when she didn't draw attention to herself. She always held her tongue and her emotions in check.

Now that she'd found a new identity in Christ, however, she spoke her mind more often. But she still felt lingering shame and disapproval from her parents, who had turned their backs on her when Lane left her—

And from the balding man now driving past them in a white luxury sedan. Everest Sloane. She didn't see him around town much, which was good, because Lane's stepfather treated her the same way her parents did.

"The people who are most important to us know the truth," Thatcher continued, pulling her attention back. "I told Dutch and Beatie last night."

"I'm telling Olivia when I see her later today." She resolved to focus on the people who cared about her and forget about Everest and her parents and anyone who might look down on her, so she could be present in the moment with Thatcher. After all, they had a wedding to plan. Fast.

He led her down the sidewalk toward his truck, but before they reached it, he stopped. "Here we are."

She did a double take at the shop windows. "The jewelry store?"

"We've got to have rings, Bliss. For Juniper as much as for us. Honoring tradition is important."

He had a point. She would be sure to find something inexpensive, however.

Once they were inside the store, a graying salesclerk in a burgundy tie showed them a display of engagement rings. Thatcher leaned the butts of his hands on the countertop and stared down into the glass case. "What do you like, Bliss?"

She leaned into him to whisper, close enough to catch a whiff of aftershave. "I thought we'd only be looking at wedding bands, not engagement rings. We're only going to be engaged for five more days."

"It's up to you, but I want you to have options."

Kind of ironic, seeing as they were getting married because they were both completely out of options.

Biting her lip, she peered at the black velvet trays of rings. The amount of sparkle was overwhelming, but—

He must have caught the way her gaze held on a simple but elegant marquise-cut diamond on an unadorned gold band, because he tapped the glass over it. "Could we see this one, please?"

The clerk handed it over, so she might as well try it on.

And then she had to blink to keep the tears at bay.

"What's wrong?" Thatcher leaned sideways against the counter. "If you hate that one, try another."

That wasn't the problem at all. "I don't hate it."

"Ah." His lips twitched. "It's pretty, Bliss."

"It is."

"And it's perfect on your hand, like it was made just for you."

"It's the right size and everything." She wished she didn't like it so much, but it was precisely the style of ring she always imagined when she was a girl.

"Do you want to try another on?" She could hear the smile in his voice.

She shook her head. "I don't need this. I'm fine with a plain band, Thatcher."

"You deserve better than fine, Bliss. And this will be on your finger for a long time."

A long time… It was hard to think further ahead than Saturday's wedding.

Half an hour later, they left the shop. Thatcher carried a small white bag holding the gold bands they would exchange during the ceremony. The solitaire diamond on her finger caught the bright sunlight and cast shimmers over her coat. “It really is a lovely ring, isn’t it?”

“It’s beautiful.” But Thatcher wasn’t looking at her hand. He was smiling at her, his gaze on her face, as if he enjoyed the pleasure she was taking in it.

Her heart quickened and her gaze locked back on the ring. “The prettiest ring I’ve ever seen. Thank you.”

“Thank *you*. You’re helping me keep my home, Bliss. And I’d do anything to ensure Juniper stays with you, as she ought to. So maybe we should stop thanking each other.”

“That doesn’t sound very polite of us, if we never thank each other for the rest of our lives.” She couldn’t help but tease.

“I meant about our arrangement.” Chuckling, he opened the passenger-side door of his truck for her with a flourish.

“I know. And in all seriousness, I’m grateful for all you’ve done for me and Juniper. The fact that you consider her feelings in all of this means a lot.” She slid into the truck and looked down at the ring on her finger.

And realized something.

Since they were following certain traditions for Juniper’s sake, then Bliss ought to make sure they followed a few others. Like dressing the part.

After school, she showed Juniper her engagement ring, and then drove straight back to Main Street, sliding the SUV into a parking spot in front of Vivienne’s Dresses. It was the nicest clothing store in town, and hopefully, they’d carry something in Juniper’s size, too.

A sporty red sedan pulled into the spot beside her. A

woman with short dark hair and bright green cats-eye sunglasses hopped out and waved.

"Olivia's here," Juniper exclaimed.

"I asked her to join us." Her call to inform Olivia about her impending marriage hadn't gone as well as Bliss had hoped, so she thought some face time might not hurt. In addition, Olivia was concerned about Juniper, which Bliss appreciated, but maybe seeing firsthand how happy Juniper was would set Olivia at ease.

"Hi, kiddo." Olivia hugged Juniper, patted Coco and gaped at Bliss's ring.

"Come on." Juniper tugged Vivienne's door open.

"Welcome in. How may I help you ladies?" With her cropped gray curls and welcoming expression, the store clerk reminded Bliss of a great-aunt she had loved as a child.

"My foster mom is getting married," Juniper announced before Bliss could say anything. "And we need dresses."

"Not me," Olivia added. "I'm just lending support."

The smiling woman's hand went to her heart. "Congratulations to the bride. Unfortunately, I do not carry bridal couture."

"It's a small wedding. Something I could wear again for Easter would be wonderful."

Juniper held up a hot-pink sequined number with a prom-like vibe. "This would be good for my bridesmaid dress, don't you think, Bliss? And for Easter, too."

Not quite appropriate for Juniper's age, to Bliss's thinking, but she smiled anyway. Her foster daughter still enjoyed playing dress-up on occasion, and she couldn't resist anything that sparkled. Juniper was obviously enjoying every second of this.

"I don't think it comes in your size, but you may try it for fun, if you like." Bliss glanced around, but unfortunately, the shop didn't appear to carry preteen sizes. "It looks like we'll have to go somewhere else for your dress, but we'll do that next, okay?"

"I might be able to help with that, too." The clerk's eyes twinkled. "Come with me." She led them to the back corner, where three shell-pink velvet armchairs sat facing a changing area. "You, my dear, may try this on now, if you like." She hung the hot-pink gown in a curtained cubicle for Juniper. "You two, please have a seat and I'll bring you a few things to look at. Would you care for water? The dog, too?"

"Thank you, but we brought our own water bottles. Even Coco has one." Bliss pulled them out, but her gaze followed Juniper as she ran into the dressing room. "Want some help?"

"No thanks." Juniper waited for Coco, then closed the drape.

"Well, Juniper does seem happy, Bliss, but she's a child," Olivia whispered. "I still think you're rushing into this."

"I agree there, but I can't adopt her without a stable income. I'm all she has, and I am marrying for her sake. Not mine." Bliss opened Coco's travel bottle and set it on the floor so it would be ready when they came out. "I know Thatcher, too. He means what he says."

"Does he?"

"What's that supposed to mean?"

"Thatcher has a reputation. Never commits to one woman, though there have been many who tried and failed."

Bliss had broached the same topic with Thatcher back in Natalie's kitchen, and she well recalled Tammy's appraisal back at the diner. "He and I have discussed it. That's in his past. You've seen him at church. You know he's not like that now."

Olivia shook her head, but Bliss took it with a grain of salt. Olivia had never healed from the pain inflicted by the man she once loved.

"I'm grateful for your honesty, Liv, but it will be okay."

"I'll always support you. You know that. But it sure seemed like Thatcher was following in the footsteps of his womanizing uncle. I don't think I could ever trust a man like that."

A man who'd turned to God and repented? "That's not fair, Olivia."

The cubicle curtain flew open and Juniper emerged, hands in the air. The oversized dress trailed the ground behind her. "Ta-da!"

Bliss clapped. "Stunning."

"Unforgettable," Olivia agreed.

The clerk returned with three pastel dresses over her arm. "I ordered these for my granddaughters for Easter, but it occurred to me they're about your size, young lady, and there's plenty of time for me to order a replacement for my girls if you decide you like one. Care to try one on?"

Juniper rubbed a gossamer, pale blue sleeve between her fingers. "Yes, please. They look more wedding-y than the one I'm wearing does, I think."

"I think you're right." The clerk gave Bliss a surreptitious wink.

The next half hour passed in a pleasant blur, as long as Bliss blocked out Olivia's concerns. Her friend meant well, and Bliss was grateful for her honesty, but her choice was made.

While Bliss assisted Juniper with one of the new dresses, the clerk—who turned out to be Vivienne herself—filled a second dressing room for Bliss with three complete ensembles: dresses, shoes, necklaces and even undergarments.

"Whoa." Juniper marveled at the items Vivienne had chosen for Bliss. "Is this what Cinderella felt like?"

Bliss struggled for words. "It might be."

Vivienne patted her arm. "Every woman should feel like a princess at least once in her life."

"Which should I try first? The peach floral?" It would make a solid church dress once the wedding was over. "Or the blue one?"

"Nuh-uh. The creamy one." Juniper pointed at the dress hanging on the center peg.

"Agreed." Even Olivia looked impressed by it.

It wasn't the most practical of the three, but seeing it like this?

Maybe it was the talk of Cinderella, but Juniper was right. There was something special about this dress, and she couldn't ignore the pull she felt toward it. Bliss reached behind the dress to unfasten the buttons. "Here goes nothing."

A short time later, Bliss, Olivia and Juniper left Vivienne's with garment bags slung over their arms. Even Coco had a doggy smile on her sweet face. Bliss smiled down at Juniper. "Do you like your dress?"

"You know I do." Her grin widened. "Is that Mr. Thatcher?"

Sure enough, Thatcher approached them, but he hadn't seen them yet. His features were hard, and his hands were clenched at his side as he walked.

Then he met Bliss's gaze, as if caught by an invisible hook. The firm set of his jaw relaxed, and all traces of frustration fled. Later, away from their current audience, she would have to ask him what had caused him such concern.

"Hey, Junebug." Thatcher gave her a one-armed hug, then smiled at Olivia. "Hello, Olivia."

"Hi, Thatcher." Olivia studied him as if she could see inside his brain.

He grinned at Bliss. "Fancy meeting you downtown again."

"We got dresses for the wedding." Juniper clutched her garment bag to her chest. "Bliss's dress is so pretty."

Thatcher's charming grin widened. "I can't wait to see it."

"You don't need to dress up," Bliss noted.

"Maybe I want to."

The way his grin pulled up higher on one side almost looked flirtatious. Her heart took off at a gallop.

Coco's whine tugged Bliss back to reality. Fast.

She turned. Juniper was standing, smiling, but Coco pawed at her leg. Bliss's heart jumped into her throat. "Coco's warning us. A seizure might be coming."

Olivia grabbed the dresses from their arms. Bliss reached to guide Juniper to a safer location than the sidewalk, but Thatcher was faster.

He scooped Juniper into his powerful arms, holding her close. "Everything will be all right, Junebug." His demeanor was calm, but the look in his eyes told Bliss he understood that every second counted. "Tell me what to do."

"Follow me." Praying, she ran back to Vivienne's.

The following two hours at Goldenrod's Urgent Care clinic had felt like the longest of Thatcher's life, but Juniper was home now. Almost, anyway. Thatcher gathered Juniper from the back seat of his truck and carried her into Bliss's house.

He had never been here before. The house in the pear orchard might need some updates, but it was homey and warm, awash in the soft light of table lamps that must have been set to timers. The mouthwatering aromas of meat and barbecue sauce swirled through the air, reminding him he hadn't eaten since lunch at Trixi's.

But food wasn't as important as the bundle in his arms. "Where should I set you down, Junebug?"

"The couch, please," Juniper murmured into his chest. "I don't want to go to bed yet. I want to stay out here with you."

At Bliss's nod, Thatcher crossed the living room and set Juniper atop the plush beige couch.

Bliss promptly covered Juniper with a blanket crafted from thick, cream yarn. "Comfy? Warm enough?"

Juniper's nod morphed into a wide yawn.

Coco sniffed around Juniper as if to ensure she was safe, and then the dog turned her large eyes to Bliss.

Bliss switched her attention from her foster daughter to the Labrador, rubbing the dog's ears and then removing the blue service vest. "Such a good girl, Coco. Well done. You must be hungry. We all missed dinner, didn't we?"

At the word *dinner*, Coco's eyes widened comically, but Thatcher admired her refusal to leave Juniper's side.

"Where's her food?" Thatcher kept his voice low since Juniper's eyes were closed.

"The pantry," Juniper murmured before Bliss could respond. "Coco gets one and a half scoops, and don't forget to clip the bag closed when you're done, so pests don't get in it. And be sure to give her a treat because she takes such good care of me."

Thatcher's heart shifted in his chest. This sweet girl had endured a lot in her short life, but even in her weary state, her concern was for Coco. "Got it, Junebug."

He smoothed her hair back from her brow, then strode the short distance to the kitchen, Coco dancing at his heels.

As he washed up at the chipped kitchen sink, Bliss pulled two white plates from the cupboard. "It'll just be us for dinner. Juniper is depleted after a seizure and will probably sleep until morning. I'll move her later."

"Sure." One and a half scoops of kibble later, Thatcher set Coco's stainless steel dish atop a black feeding mat. Tail wagging, Coco stared at Bliss instead of diving into the food.

"Take it," Bliss said, and at the command, Coco tucked into her kibble.

Thatcher shook his head in amazement. "She is the best-trained dog I've ever seen. And Mick has introduced me to some amazing animals before." As a veterinarian, Mick had found homes for several retired service and therapy animals.

"I can't imagine how we'd function without Coco." Bliss removed two large forks from a drawer. "Do you mind opening a jar of pickles while I shred the pork? It's in the cupboard right by your head."

"You've got it."

Her kitchen was almost as small as his, but he liked it far better. Maybe it had something to do with the vintage decor—some of which he suspected had belonged to her grandfather, and others which reflected her taste, such as the small cordless lamps on the countertops where the light from the overhead fluorescents didn't quite reach. Regardless, he felt at home, working beside her in the kitchen as Coco devoured her supper…which reminded him of something that had crossed his mind while they were waiting for the doctor at the clinic.

"I didn't realize Coco could warn you if a seizure is coming."

"Technically, she doesn't. She's a Seizure *Response* Dog, trained to whine or bark for help when a seizure happens, and then stay with Juniper. She'll even lie atop Juniper if a seizure is violent, to protect her." Bliss set out a package of fluffy buns beside the plates. "But after a few months, Coco started to whine right before a seizure happened. We don't know if Coco notes a change in Juniper's demeanor or smells a biochemical change, but however she does it, I'm grateful."

"That's an incredible blessing, to have a warning like that."

"Boy, is it. Sometimes Juniper notices a weird taste in her mouth before a seizure, but that didn't happen this time. Without Coco, she could have fallen on the sidewalk. Generalized tonic-clonic seizures can come on fast."

"I saw that firsthand." And he didn't like it one bit. "I can see why it's difficult to let Juniper out of your sight."

Her gaze darted through the kitchen's open floor plan into the family room, where Juniper still curled up on the couch. "Coco has made a huge difference. I have a sense of reassurance knowing she's watching over Juniper when I'm not with her. She's also given Juniper more confidence at school, and Juniper doesn't feel as isolated from other kids as she did when she first moved in with me."

"Coco deserves a medal."

"And every doggy treat we can buy for her, but the thing is, she only wants one thing. To be with Juniper."

Sure enough, once the last bite of kibble was in her mouth, Coco trotted into the family room. Juniper's eyes didn't open, but her hand snaked out from beneath the blanket to touch Coco's head.

Desire to protect that little girl burned in Thatcher's

chest. Nothing would get in the way of Bliss's adoption or Juniper receiving the best medical treatment available. Not if he had anything to do about it.

But for the moment, he needed to take care of Juniper's mom. "Do you want the pickles on the table?"

"Right here is fine. I thought we could serve ourselves from the Crock-pot." She pulled a coleslaw kit from the refrigerator. "It's nothing fancy."

"It's perfect."

A few minutes later, they sat beside each other at the table, in the open area between the kitchen and the family room. They had a perfect view of Juniper, whose breathing was now even and deep.

Thatcher offered grace and they tucked in. "This is amazing. When I have a long or rough day, I rarely eat anything better than a frozen pizza."

"But you're such a good cook."

"Mainly when I have someone to cook for. Which I do now." He tipped his head at Juniper. "How often does she suffer seizures?"

Bliss took a sip of water. "It depends. Her epileptologist is wonderful, but finding the perfect dosage of the perfect medicine for each individual is a complicated process. We have to be patient, but sometimes it feels like we're throwing cooked noodles at a wall to see what sticks."

Thatcher had sat by while Bliss and the urgent care pediatrician consulted with Dr. Cruz, Juniper's specialist at the children's hospital in San Diego, over video chat, and it had been quite an educational experience. "I have so much to learn. I knew all of this had to be difficult for you both, just as head knowledge. But now that I've had a small taste of what you two go through?"

"It's not me. Juniper's the one bearing the burden. And

oh, is she strong. I marvel at her every day." Bliss hesitated, then stared down at the engagement ring on her finger. "But I have to ask, now that you've seen what our life can be like. Are you sure this is what you want, Thatcher? I'd rather know now than a year into this."

The saucy pork went bitter on his tongue.

"Bliss?" Juniper stirred.

"Yes, sweetheart." Bliss hopped from her chair.

"I'm ready for bed."

"I've got this." Thatcher scooped Juniper in his arms and carried her down the hall, following Bliss's instructions, then kissed the little girl goodnight.

"Sleep well, sweetheart."

While Bliss assisted Juniper, Thatcher let Coco out back, then returned to the kitchen. Making himself at home, he filled the sink with hot, soapy water and started on the dishes. He was rinsing the plates when he heard Bliss let Coco inside.

A minute later, she joined him in the kitchen. "Wow, you're pretty much done. Thank you. Not just for the dishes, but for everything today. I truly appreciate you going with us to the doctor and staying for dinner."

He couldn't imagine *not* doing those things, but he could read a wariness in her eyes as if she expected to be let down. It made him wonder yet again what sort of man her former husband had been. And reminded him of the conversation they'd been having when Juniper stirred from the couch.

"You asked me a few minutes ago if I'm still sure about marrying you, Bliss. I am."

"I know you need a wife to keep the ranch, but…" She shrugged and turned away.

"What?"

She tugged a dish towel from the oven door handle. "At urgent care, the medical assistant seemed to know you."

Oh, that. He unstopped the sink. "It's a small town."

"Did you date her?"

He let out a long sigh. "A few years ago."

She began drying the salad bowl. "I just wondered if you'd rather marry someone like her since you seemed to have shared something."

"No, Bliss. I was a different man back then. I am not my Uncle Asa." They might be related, but Thatcher had no intention of turning out like him.

"I didn't mean to make you uncomfortable by bringing that up. But it seemed like Tammy at the diner knew you, too."

"She knows everyone who eats at the diner. Bliss, in case it's not clear—" Thatcher stood in front of her and cradled her soft cheek in his hand "—I'm going to be faithful. I want to be a godly man, and I take marriage seriously. Even if what you and I share is not a 'real' marriage. It's real enough as far as my commitment to you and Juniper goes."

Her eyes were weary, but shining with sincerity. "I appreciate your devotion to God and your intention to be loyal to me."

"We're going to be a family. If you haven't changed your mind, that is."

"No." Her voice was soft as a breath. "Thank you for sticking with us."

He caught himself brushing her cheek with his thumb—a definite no-no, so he dropped his hand and rinsed down the sink. He mustn't forget he was marrying Bliss for the sake of Foxtail Ranch. For his future.

For Bliss and Juniper's futures.

He was a family man now. Something he never thought he'd be.

But he didn't dare care about Bliss more than that.

He might not even be capable of love. Not like that. So he mustn't touch her like that again. Must not even put the idea of it in either of their minds.

Chapter Five

Valentine's Day dawned clear and cold, so Bliss tugged her seldom-used dress coat from the hall closet. The knee-length garment of beige wool smelled of cedar, triggering memories of past occasions when it had been worn.

Like the Christmas Eve service at church. And, stretching further back, her birthday eight years ago, when she and Lane had attended a play.

She didn't want to think about her late husband today. She didn't have time to, anyway, with Thatcher on his way. She pulled Juniper's coat from the closet. "About ready, sweetheart?"

"I'm still putting on my shoes," Juniper called from her bedroom.

"Oh, Coco, what happened?" The ribbon around Coco's neck perfectly matched Juniper's dress, but it was coming undone. Bliss squatted, tucking Juniper's coat beneath one arm as she remedied the situation.

Juniper danced out of her room, twirling so the frothy blue hem of her dress twisted around her calves. "What's Thatcher wearing today?"

"I don't know, but we'll soon find out." She handed the coat to her foster daughter.

"I can't wait. I just wish the wedding were here in town so all of our friends could come."

Considering this marriage was a legal arrangement rather than a romantic one, Bliss felt more comfortable keeping the ceremony small. She was nervous enough as it was, without being watched by their family and friends. Olivia and Thatcher's cousins were well-meaning, but it was clear they still weren't completely on board with her and Thatcher's choice to marry.

But she completely understood Juniper's desire for a larger celebration. "At least we'll get to see your grandma, and have a fancy lunch out. You look gorgeous, and so does Coco."

Juniper struck a funny pose, and as Coco's tail wagged, Bliss caught a whiff of the doggy shampoo they'd used on her last night.

Juniper reached up to adjust a lock of Bliss's hair. "You do, too, Bliss."

"Thanks." Although she hadn't put a lot of effort into preparing herself this week. She'd been too busy packing their things to move into the rental cottage at Foxtail Farm. Thanks to Thatcher's strong arms and the dry, sunny weather, it had all gone well.

Of course, she wasn't moving everything she and Juniper owned. They would only be at the rental cabin until the ranch house was ready, and even then, there was no need to clean out her grandfather's farmhouse. Thatcher had agreed to move back here, after all.

Coco's ears perked up, and Bliss wasn't surprised to hear Thatcher's truck rumbling up to the house a few moments later.

"He's here." She scooped up her purse and Coco's pink

bag. When she swung the front door open, Thatcher was already getting out of his truck.

"G'morning, Thatcher." Juniper raced down to meet him while Bliss locked the door. "What's that behind your back?"

Curious, Bliss turned around as she shoved the key into its special pocket in her purse.

And then she gasped out loud.

To say that Thatcher cleaned up well was an understatement. He had taken obvious care with every aspect of his appearance, from his thick, dark hair down to his western boots. The cut of his blue suit emphasized his muscular frame, and the white shirt and tie added a sense of formality to his appearance. He looked like, well, a groom. And a very handsome one, at that.

If that weren't enough, his expression was tender. Almost expectant, as if there was nowhere else in the world this burly, strong rancher would rather be than with Bliss and her little girl and a Labrador. His gaze swept over them, and he broke into a wide grin. "Wow, you ladies look beautiful."

Oh, how it sounded like he truly meant it. None of the men in her life had ever really seemed to mean it when they rarely uttered similar words to her, more like obligatory platitudes.

Maybe that was why Thatcher's words hit her straight in the solar plexus. Her heart began a rapid gallop that she could hear in her ears. Surely the rest of the world could hear it, too, but then Juniper squealed, thankfully drowning out everything else.

Before she could thank him and return the compliment, he revealed the bouquets he'd been holding behind his broad back, one of red roses, and the other, pink.

"Two bouquets? Is one for *me*?"

"Sadie arranged these pink ones special for you." He opened the back door of the cab for her. "A bridesmaid deserves a bouquet, doesn't she?"

"No one ever gave me roses before. And there are plushies in the truck!" Juniper almost screamed.

"One for you, one for Coco, and there are chocolates for Bliss and your grandma, too. Happy Valentine's Day."

"Thank you, Thatcher." Juniper's hug for him was fierce but short as she launched herself into the truck. "They're so cuuuute! Look, Coco! There's a lambie for you."

Coco instantly clamped the stuffed animal in her jaws.

Bliss accepted the roses from Thatcher, relishing their sweet perfume. "These are beautiful. Thank you for the gifts. But I don't have anything for you." She hadn't so much as thought of acknowledging the holiday with him. They weren't exactly valentines.

"I didn't expect anything."

"Still… I'll pick up a doughnut for you later."

"I won't say no to that." Laughing, he opened her car door.

As they descended the winding road to the valley floor, Bliss focused on calming her nerves, and she felt much better by the time they reached the interstate a half hour later. The next forty minutes or so passed in a blur of conversation and commenting on the winter-green landscape. When Thatcher exited the freeway, Juniper regaled them with details from yesterday's Valentine's party at school.

"Those were always so fun," Bliss said. "I loved decorating cereal boxes for my classmates to put valentines in."

"Did you like that, too, Mr. Thatcher?" Juniper leaned forward in her seat. "Can I call you Thatcher now instead of mister?"

"Absolutely." Thatcher grinned. "And no, I did not love

making those lace doily mailbox monstrosities, but I always felt it was worth it to get the cookies at the end of the party."

"Would you have preferred decorating your cereal box with flannel or burlap?" Bliss teased, but then Thatcher pulled up to a large white Victorian-era house and a thrill of nervous energy killed her sense of humor. Things were about to get real. "This is it, huh?"

"Looks like it." Thatcher set the parking brake. "A couple runs it out of their home and rents out the yard for receptions and parties. I can see why. It's a great house. It reminds me of your grandpa's house."

"If I did thousands of dollars in renovations, maybe." She scanned the pitched roof and decorative trim. "I love the gingerbread, though. This is giving me ideas."

"Come on, let's do this." Juniper unbuckled her seat belt. Coco's tail wagged. And Bliss, now that the moment could no longer be avoided and nervousness threatened to overwhelm her, clutched her bouquet of red roses for dear life.

As they strode up the walk bisecting a well-kept lawn, a couple in bridal clothes stepped out onto the porch, giggling. Bliss exchanged glances with Thatcher, who appeared more amused than nervous. How was he not shaking in his fancy boots?

They stepped into a wood-paneled foyer where a woman with fluffy brown bangs stood behind a walnut desk. "Do you lovebirds have an appointment?"

Bliss's tongue tied in a knot as she struggled with how to answer. Yes, to the appointment, no to the lovebirds. Thankfully, Thatcher gave the woman a smooth smile. "Thatcher Dalton."

"I'm Arnelle, and Craig is—Craig?" She called over her shoulder. "The eleven o'clock is here."

A lean man in a gray suit that matched the hue of his

thick hair appeared from the hall. "Excellent. Let's get you started on the paperwork. This way."

They followed him into a small parlor and sat on a hard couch that looked old enough to have served the house's original occupants. Bliss and Thatcher furnished the required documents and filled out a form. Once Thatcher provided his credit card, Arnelle reappeared with a camera in hand. "This way, please."

Bliss had assumed they would marry in front of the fireplace here, but Arnelle took them into an even larger parlor. Instead of period-piece furnishings, this room featured rows of white folding chairs. The fireplace in the front of the room was decorated with floral swags and arrangements, creating a pretty backdrop for photos.

Bliss paused by one of the chairs, setting down her bouquet, Coco's backpack and her purse so she could remove her coat. Juniper was faster with her jacket, and she spun in a circle to make the skirt twirl.

"Look, Thatcher. Isn't it pretty?"

"Beautiful, Junebug." There was a gruff tone to his voice, and Bliss's head jerked up. But there was no trace of vexation on his chiseled features, only a pull like gravity as he stared at her. "You look stunning, too, Bliss."

Her heart did that loud galloping thing again, reverberating through her body, but this time, she had to speak around the pounding in her throat. "Thank you. You do, too."

It came out half strangled. Hiding her face, she turned to grab her bouquet.

Craig held out his arms, inviting them closer. "Shall we begin?"

Thatcher wasn't the least bit nervous. This was actually sort of fun. Juniper seemed to be enjoying herself, too. She stood at Bliss's side, and Coco sat behind her like a second bridesmaid, her mouth open in a contented expression.

Arnelle snapped a photo of Coco. "She's happy about the wedding, isn't she?"

"We all are." Juniper stroked Coco's neck.

Craig opened a black book. "We are gathered here today for the union of Thatcher Dalton and Bliss Anderson."

He gave a few remarks on marriage and then shifted into the traditional vows, which Thatcher was grateful to get through without flubbing. He wanted his sincerity to be evident in his words, his tone and even his eyes.

Bliss sounded a little quieter than usual when she repeated her vows, as if she, too, were focused on the solemnity of their promises.

"By the powers vested in me by the state of California, I pronounce you husband and wife." Craig wiggled his eyebrows. "You may now kiss the bride."

Thatcher had known this was coming. It was part of the ceremony, but he didn't want to make it weird or awkward. So, he bent and grazed his lips over hers, the contact fleeting as the brush of a feather.

As he lifted his head, however, he couldn't help wondering what it would be like to have lingered there a moment longer.

A minute longer, even—

"Hooray!" Juniper's arms wrapped around both his and Bliss's waists, pushing them together. "Family hug!"

The first of many, he expected. Thatcher wrapped an arm about each of their shoulders, and it felt a lot more comfortable than he would have expected. Especially when Juniper giggled.

She's such a special kid, Lord. I pray I don't let her down.

Arnelle set down her camera long enough to sign her

name as a witness to the ceremony, and then she resumed taking photos of them, which she promised to email to him later. And then she was ushering them back to the foyer so she could welcome the next couple.

Juniper's mouth twisted. "That was short."

"Short and sweet," Bliss said.

"And now we get to celebrate with your grandma." Thatcher led them back to the truck and they started on the thirty-minute drive to pick up Vera for lunch. She was the only person they had invited to the wedding, but she had declined, since sitting in cars for longer than a few minutes bothered her back and hips. Lunch at a local restaurant was fine with her, though, and Thatcher was more than happy to accommodate her. He'd never met Vera, but she was Juniper's grandmother and Bliss's friend, and therefore, a VIP in his book.

The pint-sized woman with iron-gray strands in her black hair waited in the lobby of her assisted living facility, dressed head to toe in purple. "Grandma!" Juniper rushed toward her for a hug. "Thatcher brought you chocolates for Valentine's Day."

"The way to my heart." She took the chocolates and tucked them into her quilted purse. "Hi, Bliss. And this is your beau?"

"Husband now." Bliss sounded shy.

"Oh, that's right. Come here, you big lug. I'm a hugger." She opened her arms.

"Nice to meet you, Vera." Thatcher bent down for her hug. She stretched up to plant a smooch on his cheek.

Then she tugged a white tissue from the depths of her sleeve. "For the lipstick I left behind. But Valentine's Day is big for kisses, you know."

"I've had plenty from Coco," Juniper said.

Any more talk of kissing and Thatcher would be thinking about the tiny brush he and Bliss exchanged, and how it sparked an awareness in him of how much he wanted to do it again.

Never would, of course, but he shouldn't even entertain the idea. In fact, the only thing he should be thinking about was taking these lovely ladies out to lunch. He smiled down at Vera. "Shall we go?"

Brunch at the small steak house was lively, with celebratory chocolate cake for dessert. It lasted just long enough for Vera to enjoy herself without growing too physically uncomfortable, and they were stuffed when they returned to her room at the facility. After another half hour of conversation and another lipstick-laden kiss on his cheek, they piled back into the truck.

The lingering clouds had disappeared, and the blue sky and bright sunlight were like a promise of spring. The drive back to Goldenrod was as speedy and as full of chatter as the drive down had been.

"Thanks for including Vera today." Bliss turned to look at him.

"She's part of our family." He pulled into Foxtail Farm's parking lot, the closest to the rental cabin—their new home. "And I'm glad she could see Juniper in her pretty dress."

"I'm going to wear it again for Easter," Junie announced from the back seat. "I'll swirl around in it and make my new Easter wish."

Was Easter wishing a new thing? "Like a birthday wish?"

"Sort of. My mom and I used to make them before she went to heaven. They're not real, but I wished for a family and now I have one."

Her statement hit him in the gut. *I will never take this*

lightly, Lord, but I know I'll need Your help to be the father figure she deserves.

They stepped out of the truck. Coco carried her new lamb plushie in her mouth and waited patiently for them to gather their belongings. The afternoon had grown so warm, Bliss and Juniper no longer needed their coats. He took them, Coco's bag and Juniper's new stuffed animal while they carried their bouquets.

"You look like a dad, carrying our things." Juniper giggled.

"In this suit?" Thatcher struck a pose. "A stylish dad."

"Very stylish," Bliss agreed with a grin.

"Not for long, though. This is T-shirt weather."

"A little early to be this warm, but it won't last." Bliss gazed at the sky as they rounded the final curve before they reached the cabin in the clearing. "I think the weather app said it would frost again next week, which I know is good for the apple trees—"

"Surprise!"

Thatcher grunted. Bliss jumped like she was coming out of her skin.

And Juniper ran ahead. "A party! Hooray!"

Coco trotted after her, plushie in her mouth, toward the cluster of friends and family gathered on the grass and applauding.

"Woohoo to the newlyweds!" Beatie waved both hands as if she held invisible pompoms, and her miniature service horse, Gidget, had a pink ribbon tied in her fluffy mane.

The clearing had been transformed into a festive reception area, with round tables topped with white cloths, flickering candles and jars of white flowers. White globe lights that echoed the pearls on Bliss's necklace hung between the pines and skirted the protective canopies sheltering a buffet table and a three-tiered cake that, despite Thatcher's irritation, looked delicious.

But it was too much. Thatcher shoved his forefinger beneath his tie and gave it a good tug.

Air. I need air.

"I thought you loved a good party," Bliss said through a strained smile.

"Sure, when I'm not the center of attention."

"It won't be that bad."

No. They would receive hugs and well-wishes. Bliss and Juniper deserved a celebration to remember. But Thatcher also expected comments and questions about their hasty wedding. Even his own family had been wary and not overly supportive. He could shrug off speculation and gossip, but could Bliss?

He wrapped a protective arm around her shoulders as they entered the fray.

Chapter Six

Within thirty minutes, Bliss had hugged almost everyone in attendance, receiving their good wishes or, in Olivia's case, a look that said *I'll be here for you if this goes south.*

She lost sight of her coat, purse and bouquet, but she never lost sight of Juniper, who had made a beeline to her friend Zoe. And Thatcher never left her side. She wished she could hold his hand, but her arms had to be free to receive the swift embraces from the guests.

Next up, Mick and Wyatt. Bliss hadn't forgotten their concerns about this marriage, but she smiled as they offered brief hugs.

"Congratulations, Bliss. You, too, Thatcher." Mick nodded.

Thatcher gestured at the decorations. "I've helped set up enough events at Foxtail to know how much effort went into this. Thanks, guys."

"Thank your cousins." Wyatt gestured at Natalie, Sadie and Dove mingling among the guests. "They worked their tails off to get this ready in five days. Natalie didn't send invitations out until this morning, either, so no one could ruin the surprise."

Mick shoved his hands in his pockets. "We all received a lot of shocked texts and phone calls, but people are happy for you. Look at Beatie." The orchard manager stood with her husband, Dutch, alongside Aunt Yvonne, his cousins' mom. "She's ninety percent over the moon."

Bliss tipped her head. "And the other ten percent?"

"Miffed that she wasn't the one to think of pairing you two up in the first place." Mick smirked. "You know what an incurable matchmaker she is. She has told all of us privately that you two are perfect for each other, even though she knows full well that you only did this to adopt Juniper and save the ranch."

Wyatt chuckled. "She's persistent, even though we keep telling her that you two are not the least bit interested in each other."

Bliss's heart didn't gallop this time. It seemed to stop altogether.

"Hey, Pastor Luke." Wyatt shifted his gaze behind Bliss's shoulder.

Thatcher turned to extend his hand to the pastor. "Thanks for coming."

"I'm honored to have been invited. Quite a surprise all around for you and for all of us guests, too."

A hot flush of embarrassment rose up from Bliss's core. "I'm sorry we didn't ask you to perform the ceremony. We didn't want a big fuss."

"Understandable." His tone was gentle, and his eyes were soft. "But while the wedding might be over, your marriage is just beginning. I'm available if you'd ever like to go through the premarital materials that I offer to couples. It's never too late to build the foundation of your family on Jesus."

"That sounds helpful." But Bliss felt like a fraud. Their marriage wasn't going to be normal by any stretch of the imagination.

"There was something else I wanted to talk to you about, Bliss." As Thatcher and Wyatt stepped away, Pastor Luke rubbed his hands together. "Are you still willing to prepare the Easter baskets this year?"

With everything else going on this week, she had forgotten. "I'd be happy to."

"What's this?" Thatcher tipped his head.

"Last year I put together baskets for homebound folks who could use a little extra help. I purchase supplies and pack them up, and a team from church delivers them."

"Sounds like a great idea." Thatcher's eyes crinkled at the corners. "I'm happy to help."

"Unfortunately, we don't have all the funds I'd hoped for this year." Pastor Luke named the budget.

"We could do a fundraiser." Thatcher rubbed his chin. "Sadie raised money for the animal shelter at Christmas by selling poinsettias."

"Good idea. I'll talk to her," Bliss said.

"I love seeing teamwork like this." Pastor Luke's gray eyes sparkled. "But this is your wedding reception, so we can talk particulars later. Enjoy yourselves."

Before they could catch their breath, a woman with sleek brown hair and a bright blue pantsuit appeared at Thatcher's elbow. "Introduce me to your bride, Thatcher."

"Hi, Aunt Yvonne." Thatcher pulled her into a side hug, which she responded to with a stiff pat on his shoulder blade. Asa's ex-wife didn't seem like much of a hugger. "Bliss, meet Yvonne Dalton—Natalie, Sadie and Dove's mom."

Bliss recalled hearing at some point that Yvonne's bad memories of her marriage to Asa kept her from visiting Foxtail often. In light of that, Bliss couldn't help but be grateful for Yvonne's effort today. "Nice to meet you, and thanks for coming."

"We're family, right? Well, Thatcher is my ex's nephew by blood, not mine, but he and my girls are so close, I can't just ignore that." She peered up at Thatcher. "Where's your mom? Did she hear I was coming and 'catch a cold' or something?" She made quotation marks with her bony fingers.

Thatcher's smile tightened. "She's on a cruise, and I wish you'd believe me when I say she doesn't avoid you."

"So you say." She gave Bliss the eye. "It's always been like this. You would think that since Doreen and I were married to brothers, we would have been friends. I mean, we had babies three months apart, and you would think that would have bonded us. Maybe we could have had a joint baby shower or something. Or even a photo of us together in our maternity smocks, but nope. She'd tried so hard to have a baby, you would think she'd be over the moon to make the drive down from Los Angeles and show off her tummy, but she claimed her morning sickness was so bad she couldn't travel or receive visitors for the entire nine months."

Bliss could tell from her tone that she thought it was made up. "A friend from church had that. Hyperemesis gravid—oh, I can't remember exactly what it's called, but her morning sickness lasted all day, and it was so severe that she needed regular IV treatment because she was so dehydrated."

Yvonne's lower lip protruded. "Maybe, but I can count on one hand the number of times I've seen Doreen since then."

"You know better than anyone how difficult it was to

be married to a Dalton brother." Thatcher's tone was kind, but firm.

"True. Just being at Foxtail makes me tense." Yvonne looked at the trees and mountains, grimacing as if they hemmed her in. "I hope you're happier living here than I was, Bliss."

"I will be." That seemed an easy promise to make.

"I'll make sure of it," Thatcher added.

Bliss mimed wiping sweat from her brow once Yvonne stalked off. "Phew."

Thatcher turned his back on the rest of the party. "I'm sorry. I wish Yvonne could have said congratulations like everyone else."

"It's fine. I feel sorry for her. It sounds like your Uncle Asa had quite a few things in common with Lane, like leaving their wives for greener pastures. It would be easy to become bitter after what she went through. I might have, if I didn't have God in my life now."

"I'm not going to do that to you, Bliss. The only greener pastures I'm interested in are on the other side of my north fence." He rubbed his forehead. "I don't want to be like Uncle Asa. Or my dad. Their families were never their top main concerns. Asa prioritized this land. My dad was all about music. Not that those things are bad, but they forgot every other obligation they had. Every promise they made. And while I may have married you to keep the land, which is a bit too much like Asa for my tastes, I want the best for you and Juniper. I won't ignore her or forget her birthday parties or—"

"Your dad forgot your birthday?"

"He usually called, but not always. Uncle Asa usually forgot, too, but one year, when I was just a bit older than Juniper, I had enjoyed a great summer at Foxtail. I spent every summer of my youth here, you know, probably so my mom didn't have to worry about childcare. Anyway, Uncle Asa was a lot of fun. I invited him to my birthday party. He promised he'd be there."

Her heart ached. "He didn't come, did he?"

"It wasn't anything worse than what his own daughters experienced with him. Those Dalton men were deadbeats." He made a scoffing sound. "Great wedding conversation. Sorry."

"I asked. But pretty soon, I'm guessing we'll be asked to cut the cake and pose for photos." She turned to follow Juniper's progress across the grass. "Poor Coco hasn't had a break in a while."

"I'll take care of it."

"Where are you going?" Olivia approached with Sadie and Mick, phones in hand. "We want pictures, and you two look nice beneath this tree."

Bliss waved her hand. "Coco needs some time off."

Mick shoved his phone in his pocket. "I've got her. I'll send Juniper this way for photos."

"There are toys and water in the pink bag, wherever it is." Bliss looked around for her purse. "Has anyone seen it?"

Oliva gestured behind her. "I set them at the table closest to the cake."

Bliss stepped closer to Thatcher for the photo. "Before I forget, I need to talk to you about a floral fundraiser, Sadie."

"Sure, but right now, give me some smiles." Sadie held up her phone.

Although they stood close together, Thatcher breached the gap between them and pulled Bliss to his side in a hug. Then he rested his head against hers.

It was a pose. She knew it. A momentary stance for a photo, not the act of a besotted husband.

But it made her feel safe and cherished. Something she hadn't felt in a long time, if ever.

Even if it wasn't real.

On the outside, she might look like Bliss Dalton, bride, mom, capable bookkeeper. But on the inside?

She was still Bliss Anderson, despised wife, daughter and daughter-in-law, who had always wanted love but only found emptiness. Any further yearning for love, aside from caring for Juniper, would lead to the same desolate place.

While she prayed for God to heal her wounded heart, she also accepted that loving Juniper was enough for her. The blessings Coco provided were enough, and so was Thatcher's friendship.

Despite how warm and comforting it was to be held against his side.

It was not in her future to be loved like that. Not in her first marriage, and certainly not in her second.

The rest of the reception wasn't bad despite Thatcher's initial qualms. Maybe because his family seemed to be over their shock over their dad creating the addendum to the will that favored Thatcher over them—for the steep price of marriage.

Maybe it was because Juniper had such a good time, laughing and twirling in her dress. Or maybe it was because Bliss was by his side throughout the whole thing, a supportive, kindred spirit through the appetizers and cutting the cake and the toast with sparkling apple cider, and so many photos his face hurt by the end of the party.

"No honeymoon," he said to everyone who asked.

They either responded with shock or a firm "Yet" or "Surely after the ranch's busy season?"

This wasn't his busiest season by a long shot, but Bliss

was adept at turning the conversation toward all the work they had to do at the ranch house. As comfortable as the rental cabin was, they couldn't stay in it for long.

To that end, he took off work Monday. While Juniper was at school, he and Bliss drove down the mountain to visit a big box home store. They selected a refrigerator, range and oven, window treatments and paint. They grabbed lunch at a sandwich shop on the way back home, and then, despite the damp weather that had settled in the night before, he took Bliss out on one of the ATVs to show her the greener grass on the other side of his north fence. The fence he wanted to tear down as soon as he got a loan so he could build a new one, extending his grazing land to the far edge of the property.

That's when he discovered the break in the wire fence. Jagged, but wide, bowed as if something had found a weak spot and exerted a fair amount of pressure on it.

Bliss shook her head. "This is big enough for a calf to get out, isn't it?"

"Yeah, and for a coyote to get in." Of all the wildlife they encountered here, coyotes were the biggest threat to his livestock. The muddy ground around the break was too wet after last night's drizzle to hold any tracks to shed more light on the subject, but thankfully, he didn't see stray fur caught in the fence or other signs of a struggle.

It didn't necessarily mean anything, though.

"I hate to cut our tour short, but I'd better handle this."

"Of course." She hopped back into the ATV, but her gaze was on the Black Angus nibbling tufts of grass in the distance. "Do you ever ride your horse out here?"

"Maverick?" The bay gelding was his favorite, but he owned a few others. "All the time, but the ATV is convenient when I've got a companion. Like Juniper."

"Thanks for bringing me today. It's lovely."

She really thought so? It shouldn't matter, but Thatcher was relieved. The ranch would be part of her life, now that they were married.

Halfway home, his cell reception improved enough to place a call to Frank, the sun-worn, fortysomething foreman. "There's a big rip in the north fence. Do you mind putting together what we need to repair it? I'll come back and pick you up for the job."

"How big is big?"

"Big enough."

"Might want to start packing bear spray. DeVoss spotted a mountain lion."

DeVoss was his neighbor on the far side of the fallow Foxtail property. "Good thing we're always on guard, but now we know to be extra cautious."

When he disconnected, Bliss was watching him. "A mountain lion sighting?"

"About a mile away. They're always active hereabouts, but let's keep Juniper close to home."

"Agreed. Speaking of home, though, look." She pointed to the other side of the eastern boundary, as if she wanted to change the subject. "I see my grandpa's trees from here. They look so sad."

"That disease hit them hard a while back." Thatcher couldn't remember which one, but the pear orchard hadn't bounced back, and her grandpa hadn't been in good enough health to replace them. Since his death and Bliss inheriting the orchard a few years ago, there hadn't been funds for her to tend it. "Do you want to plant a new orchard?"

"I never thought about it, honestly. I wouldn't know what to do. That's a problem for another day, though."

He dropped her off near the barn and met Frank. They

set back out with a trailer full of tools and patched the break.

Back at their temporary home, they tried to establish a routine. Dinner together at the table, then playtime with Coco, followed by relaxing together in the living room, Juniper with her latch-hook kit, Bliss crocheting a little purse as a gift for Olivia, and Thatcher settling with a book. Tuesday, they checked in with Juniper's case manager, but otherwise, Thatcher worked that week as usual, and Bliss began going through the file cabinets and boxes stored in the ranch house.

Their new life felt normal, like something Thatcher could get used to. He never thought he'd be a family man, but by Friday, six days into this marriage, he was rather pleased by how little he seemed to be following in his dad and uncle's footsteps.

He finished his ranch tasks by early afternoon, then turned to a few things he'd put off. He called the bank, and then added Bliss to his insurance policies. She had given him a file a week ago, and if he waited much longer, he could lose it, knowing him.

When he finished, he put on his jacket and gathered the file to return it to Bliss at the ranch house so it would be safe. Maybe he could also help her go through the boxes. She said she had finished with the file cabinets, so if he lent a hand, they could possibly clear out the house this weekend, just in time for the appliance delivery.

The day was cool and damp, but Bliss had the tuned-up heater going and the little house was snug and warm. When he opened the door she smiled at him from her spot cross-legged on the hardwood floor, surrounded by piles of paper.

"Hey, what's all this?" He shrugged out of his jacket.

"Your childhood, in a nutshell. Three boxes' worth."

"Seriously?"

She gestured at several business-sized envelopes, spread out before her. "This envelope has a lock of hair from your first trim at the barbershop. This one has some of your report cards and school certificates. Which reminds me—I need to call Juniper's school and have you put on her emergency card." She patted another banker-sized box. "This is full of photos of you. You were adorable in kindergarten."

"Thanks. But cool as all of this is, why did my dad keep my stuff here?"

"I don't think they're your dad's." She bit her lip. "These envelopes are addressed to Asa."

"My dad must have reused a few old envelopes of Asa's, then. Money was always tight."

"I get that, but the return address is your mom."

"Huh. Asa must have cared more than he let on. Where are my cousins' boxes?"

"Right there." She pointed to three ragged shoeboxes by the empty fireplace. "Maybe the rest of their childhood memorabilia is at the farmhouse." She brushed dust from her hands. "So, what brings you this way?"

"Paperwork. I added you to my medical insurance, but I wanted to get this back to you right away. By the way, you gave me Juniper's medical files, too. She's still on Medi-Cal until the adoption is final, though, correct?"

"That's right. Sorry for the confusion. I just keep our medical paperwork all together, and I forgot to mention it before handing it to you."

"No worries. It's just I wouldn't want to invade her privacy by seeing something I shouldn't. Rest assured, all I saw was basic stuff. Height, weight, blood type, that sort of thing."

"It's all good info for you to know, anyway. I can donate

to Juniper, since she and I are both O-negative. Universal donor." Bliss made jazz hands.

"Who else just told me that they were a universal donor?" He scratched the back of his neck. "Oh yeah, it was my—"

The next word froze on his tongue.

"Your what?" Bliss stood up. "Are you okay, Thatcher?"

No, he wasn't. The world had tilted on its side.

"Thatcher?" Bliss's voice went up an octave as she moved in front of him. "You're scaring me here."

Frightening her was the last thing he ever wanted to do. "I'm sorry. It's just that I understand now."

"Understand what? Help me so I can help you."

His thoughts raced too fast to put into coherent sentences, but he had to make it clear to Bliss. *Go slow and steady. Maybe it will make more sense to both of you if you do.*

"You remember learning about blood types in high school?"

"Yes. A, B, AB and O."

"We inherit an allele from each of our parents that give us our blood types. If you're O-negative, that means each of your parents gave you O genes."

"Right."

"My dad, Jake, and Uncle Asa were blood type A. Both big donors, like me, so I know that for a fact. But Dad was also Rh-negative. A-negative. I'm AB-positive."

"So then…" Bliss's face scrunched up as she thought about it. "Your mom must be B-positive, right?"

"My mom just found out she's O-negative." He could tell she hadn't followed where his thoughts had taken him. To the only credible solution. "An AB-positive child can't be born to parents whose types are A and O, both negative."

She stared at him for a full five seconds. "But then that would mean…"

Her gaze shifted, as if she fought the direction of her thoughts. Like him, she wanted it to be impossible.

But it wasn't. His sweet mother, from whom he had not inherited a single visible trait, who had raised him and soothed him and loved him with her whole heart?

It felt traitorous to speak it aloud, but the facts couldn't be disputed.

"I can't be my mom's biological child."

There was silence for a full ten seconds before Bliss blinked. "Yvonne told me your mom—Doreen—struggled to have a baby. If Doreen couldn't conceive, it's possible she and Jake visited a medical specialist."

"My parents didn't have the money for something like that. They lived hand to mouth with my dad on the road for his music, and there was nothing left when he died. And there was no other family left but Uncle Asa, who didn't have cash to help my mom, even if she had asked for it."

"Okay, maybe… I hate to suggest this, but is it possible Jake had a child—you—with another woman? And your mom raised you as her own?"

"Before Dad died, he swore to me that he was faithful to Mom, and I believed him. His left eye twitched when he fibbed, but it didn't happen that day. He was a jerk, but he kept that promise." He swallowed hard. "But Bliss, I don't think I'm Jake's son, either. Two negative blood-type parents don't have a positive blood-type kid."

"You're suggesting you're adopted?" Bliss's brow wrinkled. "I've seen photos of Asa. Everyone's right when they say you look just like him. You're a Dalton, without doubt."

"Right. It's no big deal when a nephew looks like his uncle. But when you consider how I spent every summer of my youth at Foxtail, and the blood type evidence, with all of this?"

He gestured at the mementos and photographs Asa had stored from Thatcher's childhood, a stark contrast to the shoeboxes of his cousins' childhood drawings.

He shoved down the anger whirling in his gut. "There's only one reason my mom would send this stuff to Asa. He is—was—my real father."

And Thatcher's whole life was a lie.

Chapter Seven

Bliss could only imagine how Thatcher felt at this moment, realizing the pieces of his life didn't fit together the way they were supposed to.

She had been through her share of shocking experiences, things that had knocked the wind from her lungs and left her reeling. But nothing like this.

The only thing she could think of doing to help was to offer an alternative explanation, because Thatcher didn't want to be Asa Dalton's son. And she couldn't blame him.

She reached for her purse. "Let's look at this one piece at a time, okay? There could be a reasonable explanation for the blood-type problem. Maybe there was a mutation. I'm going to look online and see if it's even possible for negative parents to have a positive child of a different blood type."

"Bliss." He turned away to stare out the window. "You don't need to do that."

"Let me try." With shaking fingers, she typed her question into the search bar. Immediately, the AI overview popped up with the answer she was hoping for. "I don't understand everything because it's a little technical, but it is possible. Rare but possible."

"How rare would it have to be for both the blood type and Rh factor to be that far off?" He didn't turn around.

"I'll keep skimming." As she read further, she bit her lip. "Do you know if your mom received a blood transfusion before you were born? Oh, I guess she would have received O-negative, though."

"You can stop looking, Bliss. I appreciate what you're trying to do, but…this is one of those situations where the most obvious answer to the riddle is the correct one."

Bliss set down her phone. "There could be other explanations."

"The facts remain. Fact number one, I'm the spitting image of Asa." He ticked off on one finger, then a second. "Fact two, I'm not Doreen's. Fact three, I can't be Jake's kid if I'm not Doreen's kid. He wasn't a good husband, but he was a faithful one. Fact four, Doreen mailed all my school photos and report cards and updates to Asa. Why would she do that? Fact five?" He held onto his pinky finger for emphasis. "Asa groomed me to take over the ranch someday, and then he left it to me as an inheritance. Because I was his kid."

She wanted to cry, but even more, she wanted to support Thatcher. *Lord, will You give me words?*

She took a deep breath. "If that's all true, that means Asa fathered a child—you—with someone while Yvonne was expecting Natalie. And he gave you to his brother and sister-in-law to adopt, and it's been a secret for your whole life."

"You heard Yvonne. My mom had trouble conceiving. If they couldn't afford to adopt, I'm sure this was a happy opportunity for them. Maybe they paid for me with their silence, who knows—but it explains why they avoided Aunt Yvonne during my mom's so-called pregnancy." His laugh was mirthless. "Aunt Yvonne is the only one who hasn't lied to me my whole life."

Bliss drew alongside him, praying for peace. "You need

to talk to Doreen. Do you want me to leave so you have privacy to call her?"

"She's on that cruise. I'm not going to ruin it for her."

"That's thoughtful, but you deserve answers."

"I need some time. I'm not as calm as I want to be when I have that conversation with her."

"I can understand that." Her hand gently rubbed small circles on his lower back.

"I don't want to tell my cousins yet, either. Maybe they should never know. It would cause so much pain."

"Secrets have a way of coming out eventually. Case in point." She gestured at the boxes. "But if Asa is your dad, why did he make things so hard on you in his will?"

"Because he knew the apple didn't fall far from the tree. He saw me grow up, watched how I dated a lot. He probably worried I was destined to be just like him and thought marriage would change me."

Bliss shook her head. "If he thought you were like him, he wouldn't push you into marriage. He would want you to avoid it."

"Maybe he didn't want me to end up alone the way he had. And he knew me, Bliss. I was heading down the wrong path because I was just like him." His chuckle was mirthless. "Like father, like son. No matter how much I don't want to be like him, I am."

Enough of this nonsense.

"I don't care what you did in your youth, Thatcher. No matter how bad it was, it's over. You have God now. Or, more accurately, God has you. When you gave your heart to Jesus, everything changed. You are not the same man you were when Asa drew up his will. You're a new creation."

"I don't deserve that."

"None of us deserve it."

"I don't deserve *you*, either." His eyes softened. "I just dropped a bomb on you. Your support—it means a lot to me."

"We're a team, right? We help each other in ways beyond me adopting Juniper and you keeping the ranch."

"You're right, and it's a blessing. But speaking of the ranch, I don't think the expansion is going to happen. I can't get the bank to return my calls."

The change of topic from his parentage drew her up short, but she knew from experience that sometimes a person needed an emotional break from a heavy conversation. She would follow his lead. "I thought you had a good meeting with the loan officer."

"The first appointment, yes, but out of the blue they informed me via email that they needed more information than I'd already provided. That was the day we bought the rings, in fact. I went back to the bank to settle the issue, but they were far less friendly. I asked to plead my case to the manager, but of course he was busy. Not sure I believe it, though."

Bliss's memories flashed back to seeing Thatcher downtown that afternoon, right after she and Juniper bought dresses. She remembered now how frustrated he had appeared. Then Juniper had suffered a seizure, and after that she had been so preoccupied with Juniper's well-being that she'd forgotten all about it.

She couldn't forget it now. There was only one bank in town, and a hunch poked at her like a foxtail weed stuck to her sock. "The manager is Everest Sloane."

"That sounds right. You know the guy?"

"You could say that." She picked at a hangnail. "He's Lane's stepfather. My former father-in-law."

Thatcher's eyes brightened. "I don't like relying on connections to get places in life, but if you come talk to him with me, at least I can get a foot in the door."

"I can't."

His brows rose. "*Can't?*"

Oh, dear. She hadn't meant to say it like that, but the thought of facing Everest made her stomach knot up.

"It wouldn't help." Understatement of the year. "He blames me for Lane's death."

Thatcher's face darkened like a thundercloud. "You didn't force that cheater to break his vows and run away from home."

"That's exactly how Everest and Monica, Lane's mom, saw it, though. I couldn't give him children, so in their view, he had no choice."

"Because you didn't have a baby?" Thatcher's tone was incredulous. "Now I really want to talk to this guy, but not about the loan."

"I can't imagine their suffering after losing Lane. Sadly, their grief was compounded by Monica's fight against cancer. She passed less than a year after Lane. Everest deserves compassion, but he doesn't want anything from me. Or to do with me." She tried to shrug it off. "But that's why you might not get a loan. He must have heard about our engagement."

"What kind of guy punishes people like that? I've never met someone so punitive."

"I have." She didn't like talking about her marriage, but maybe this would help Thatcher understand better why she couldn't advocate for him with Everest. "My parents. They set me up with Lane. Normally, I resisted their efforts to control me, but Lane seemed sweet. He was taking a job in San Diego, and I thought marrying him would allow us to do our own thing, away from our parents' influence. It didn't work like that, though. My parents moved there, too, and Lane wasn't the man I thought I'd married. He was controlling, scrutinizing everything from how many calories I ate a day to who I talked to in my college classes. I had one pair of friends, a married couple, but Lane hated them."

The thundercloud returned to Thatcher's face. "I don't like the sound of this at all. Did he hit you, Bliss?"

"No, but he did yell at me."

"Emotional and verbal abuse. I wish I'd known you then so I could have introduced Lane to my fist."

"Thatcher!"

"I know, it's not God's way, but I hate how you were treated."

"I didn't know any different, growing up the way I did. Isolated, walking on eggshells. But one day, after my second miscarriage, I dropped by the craft store for some yarn. There was a sign for a knit and crochet group, and I decided to go. And after that, I didn't feel as alone anymore."

"Good for you, but I'm sure Lane didn't like that." Thatcher glowered.

"Then one of the women invited me to Bible study at their church. I had been curious about Jesus for a while. It was Lane's tennis night, so I just went. I was nervous walking into that room, but I felt so at home, not just with the women, but with Him."

His scowl faded. "I can relate to that. It took me a long time to get there. But I had my family's support, and I know now you didn't."

"No, but I held firm. That's the only time I ever stood up for myself with them. And the last. Lane left me right after that."

"You must have been heartbroken."

"Yes, but…it's complicated." How to make him understand? "My parents took his side, and maybe they thought I would fall into despair, but instead, I started to grow into myself. I don't even look the same anymore. In fact, the only words Everest said to me after I moved back to town was to tell me he didn't like my shorter hair."

"I like your hair." Thatcher's gaze roamed the simple style, from the part down to the ends.

It almost felt like he was touching her straight locks with his fingers, rather than simply admiring them. The fine hair at the back of her nape prickled.

And she was going to stop her thoughts, right there. He had probably only paid her a compliment because he wanted to build her up. Thatcher was a kind man.

And he was on her team. But her thoughts had taken her far, far from the topic at hand.

The bank loan.

She rubbed the back of her neck. "I just thought you should have some background on Everest."

"I didn't know Lane was from Goldenrod. I never met the guy."

"You were only here during the summer when you were growing up and his family traveled during school vacations, so you missed him."

"Why did you come back to Goldenrod, if Everest is here?"

"Because I had happy memories of visiting my grandpa's house, and when he left it to me, it was like a lifeline. Does that make sense?"

"That's how I feel about Foxtail Ranch."

His eyes hardened then. His thoughts must have returned to Asa, the blood types, the boxes of his childhood memorabilia, the upheaval he must be feeling.

She took hold of his upper arms. "We are a team,

Thatcher. That means we don't have to face anything alone anymore. I'm with you while we figure out the identity of your biological parents."

"And I'm with you if you ever have to see Everest again." He stared into her eyes. "I don't want a loan from him, anyway."

"Maybe he'll still give it to you, after stringing you along for a while. And you need it to accomplish your goals at the ranch."

"Not from him, I don't. He wasn't good to you." He shifted and pulled her into an embrace. Not too close, but his hold was comforting and tender. "Thank you for telling me, though, and for your support. You don't know how much it means to me."

She wanted to sigh against his chest and burrow into his warmth for a rest.

But she mustn't, for about a hundred reasons. One of which was going to be out of school soon.

"It's almost time to pick up Juniper." Reluctantly, she stepped out of his reassuring hold.

"Want me to come with you?"

She did, but considering the way she was yearning to return to his comforting embrace, a little space from him would be beneficial.

So would a little levity. "I didn't know you were so partial to the school," she teased. "But don't worry. There are plenty of coming events for you to attend."

"I'm partial to Juniper," he countered, but he was smiling at her joke. "Thanks for making me feel better."

"I'll always try." It wouldn't be easy for Thatcher to work through the shock of Asa possibly—probably—being his father, too.

But her supportive friendship was one of the only things

she could give him. Anything more than that wouldn't just be unwelcome, but wrong, because feelings like those spreading warmth and light through her like a sunrise?

They went against their agreement. And there was no getting around it, ever.

When Bliss had said something about "coming events" at Juniper's school two weeks ago, Thatcher hadn't been sure what she meant. He was up for anything, but once he learned doughnuts were involved?

On the first Friday morning in March, a half hour before the morning bell sounded, Thatcher sat on a rock-hard bench in the school cafeteria. He had a paper cup of black coffee in one hand, a glazed doughnut in the other, and his favorite girl—plus their favorite dog—across the laminate table from him.

Over Juniper's shoulder, the cafeteria stage was decorated with posters welcoming them to Doughnuts with Dads. A few dozen kids at tables around them shared smiles and pastries with the men in their lives.

"So then—" Juniper continued her story "—Coco sat straight up in class, thinking we were talking about her, not the spelling word, but it was *c-o-c-o-a*."

"Oh no, poor baby." He reached over to rub one of Coco's silky ears. "How did she get her name, anyway?" The Labrador was black, not brown.

"All the puppies in the training group were named after fancy fashion designers. Bliss says there's Coco purses and outfits and even perfume. I want to try that when I'm old enough."

How old was old enough? Thatcher didn't know, but he was happy to have a front row seat watching this little girl grow up.

As always, the thought passed through his head that his dad, Jake, never did anything like this with him, just as Uncle Asa probably hadn't for Natalie, Sadie or Dove.

Except now that he suspected—no, he knew, deep in his bones—that Asa was his biological dad, he was more determined than ever to be nothing like Asa or Jake, too obsessed with their own interests to attend a single school play, sporting event or choir concert. With God's help, he would be more like his mom, always present, front and center. Thatcher was grateful for her, and he determined to do the same for Juniper so she would never feel the way he had as a kid.

Juniper turned her head at a pair of new arrivals to the cafeteria. "Zoe and her dad are here. Can they sit with us?"

"Of course." He waved at Zoe's dad, a stocky man with a dark buzz cut. "Care to join us, Luis?"

"We'd love to." Luis Alamilla took Juniper's seat after she switched to sit alongside Thatcher.

Zoe greeted Coco, and then the girls started chatting immediately.

Although the men weren't close, Thatcher knew Luis and his wife Bess through Mick, and it was nice to see a familiar face in the room. Thatcher lifted his cup. "This is cool, isn't it?"

"I wouldn't miss it, even though it meant switching shifts today." Luis was a member of the police department. "Not everyone has the luxury to do that, of course, which makes me all the more grateful to be here."

"I feel the same way." The school was fantastic for putting something like this on. He also appreciated the adult volunteers setting out fresh doughnuts and pouring coffee at the table closest to the stage. "Are those teachers?" Thatcher would thank them on his way out.

Luis turned over his shoulder to peek. "A few, but this was set up by the parent-teacher association. Bliss is a member. Congratulations, by the way. I heard you two got married."

"Thanks. Yeah."

"We're happy to take Juniper sometime so you two can go on a date."

Dinner out sounded fun.

Adult conversation was nice.

But a date implied romance. And after their hug in the ranch house? Thatcher was no longer thinking of Bliss as just a friend.

Their hug started out as an act of comfort. He'd been upset about Asa and the way her family—and in-laws—had treated her. But after a minute, he'd realized he didn't want to let her go. Her hair smelled like fruity shampoo, and it felt silky beneath his chin. He'd wanted to twist a strand of it around his fingers. And he'd never, ever wanted her to feel sad again.

He gulped his coffee. Thankfully it was lukewarm, or he would have burned his throat.

"That'd be great," he managed.

They chatted for several more minutes before Luis picked up his empty coffee cup. "Almost time for school. See you two later." He and Zoe rose to throw out their trash.

Thatcher tossed his crumpled napkin into his empty coffee cup "Are you finished with your hot chocolate, Junebug?"

"Two more sips." She took one. "I've never been to Doughnuts with Dads before, because my dad gave me away. I think he's in prison, but I'm not sure. Grandma hasn't heard from him since he signed me away when I was in preschool."

Juniper's words hit Thatcher like a mule kick. It took him a moment to find his breath. "It sounds like he wanted you to have the best life possible, and he knew he couldn't give it to you. Not with all of his struggles."

He should probably extend Asa the same benefit of the doubt since he, too, gave away a child, but he couldn't. It was a different situation completely. Asa wasn't an addict or incarcerated. He was a selfish man who didn't want the embarrassment of acknowledging Thatcher as his own.

But this wasn't about him right now. It was about Juniper, and making sure she never felt a moment's doubt that she was precious.

"The families we're born into are important, but family is more about heart than it is about blood. The most important family we're in is God's." He spoke to himself as much as to Juniper. "And you know what God thinks about you, Juniper Jones, don't you?"

"He made me and loves me no matter what." She fiddled with her purple epilepsy bracelet. "And He's with me all the time."

"That's right. And Bliss and I are here, too. No matter what."

She continued fidgeting with her bracelets. "Can I ask you something?"

"Anything."

The school bell rang, long and tinny, calling children to class.

"Never mind." Juniper shifted, signaling Coco to prepare to move.

But Thatcher recognized how difficult it was for her to broach the topic, so he didn't want to put her off. Praying for wisdom, he wrapped an arm around her shoulders. "We have a minute, if you want to talk now."

She stared at the floor. "You know how this is called Doughnuts with Dads?"

"Yeah?"

"Well, you're here like a dad. You do dad-type things for me, like helping me with my homework and taking me to look at calves. So I wondered if, once Bliss adopts me, if I can call you guys Mom and Dad."

Emotion flooded his core. He couldn't name the exact feeling, but it was stronger than affection, deeper than appreciation, bolder than mere happiness. It spread warmth through his limbs, stung at the back of his eyes and filled his throat so he wasn't sure he'd be able to speak properly.

He lifted her chin with the side of his forefinger. "Junebug, look at me, please."

Her lashes swept upward.

"That is the most wonderful thing anyone has ever said to me. Ever. Let's talk about it with Bliss, but I'm pretty sure what her answer will be. She'll just want to make sure that *you're* sure. This is all about you, sweetheart. Okay?"

"Okay." She rose and wrapped her arms around his waist for a hug that was as firm as it was brief. "I'd better go. I don't want to be late."

"Definitely not. Have a good day, Junebug. Praying for you." After their hug, Thatcher reached to stroke Coco's silky ears. "Take care of our girl, Coco."

Coco nuzzled his hand with her damp nose, as if acknowledging his request. Then she joined Juniper, rushing from the cafeteria.

He stared at the doorway a few seconds after she'd left, humbled by the gift Juniper had given him.

I don't deserve her, Lord.

He made his way to the parking lot and hopped into the

truck. A full day of work waited for him at the ranch, but he sat in the cab without turning on the ignition.

Now he better understood what Bliss had meant in Natalie's kitchen when he first broached getting married. *This can never be a temporary marriage.*

At the time, he had understood her words in his head. Wholeheartedly agreed with them. He cared about Juniper and never wanted her to feel uncertain or confused.

But today, he understood Bliss's words in his heart. He didn't just care about Juniper anymore. He loved her, and he would move the Cuyamaca Mountains, one shovelful of dirt at a time, to keep her safe and happy.

Fifteen minutes later, he stepped into the ranch house. Since he had cleared out the boxes, there was a lightness to the living room. It had less to do with the washed windows and more to do with the absent memorabilia his mom had sent to Asa. All those photos and report cards and elementary school art projects were reminders of who he was—or wasn't.

"Bliss?" His call echoed off the bare walls.

"In the back bedroom."

He followed the faint whiff of paint to the room Juniper had chosen. Bliss, wearing a paint-spattered gray sweatshirt and black leggings, had no idea how sweet she looked with her tongue poking out of the corner of her mouth like that. It was an unconscious habit of hers when she concentrated, whether she was tallying numbers or, in this case, brushing patches of greenish-grayish blue paint samples on the sunniest wall.

She turned to smile at him. "How were the doughnuts?"

"Excellent. So was the company." He squinted at the wall. "Those are the colors Juniper is deciding between?"

"Yep." She pointed at each swatch. "This one is Sea Glass. This is Aqua Breeze. And this is Dreamweaver."

He stroked the stubble on his chin. "They all look the same."

"Really? Dreamweaver is a lot darker—oh, you're teasing me."

He laughed.

"You're such a stinker, Thatcher." Grinning, she flicked him with a clean rag.

He wanted to grab the end of it and playfully thwack her back. But that fell into the category of flirting, which was a no-no, so he forced his attention back to the wall. "Seriously, whichever one she picks will be great. They remind me of the dress she wore to our wedding."

"Me, too." She dropped the brush into a small metal bucket half-full of water. "What brings you by?"

Before he could answer, his phone buzzed. "Just a sec. It could be Frank." The foreman might be ready to go out and inspect their repairs on the north fence.

Not Frank. He read the message and shoved his phone back into his jeans pocket.

"Everything okay?"

"It was Natalie. They want everyone to go out to brunch at Cocina Rosa after church on Sunday. They need a head count for a reservation."

"I can see why. The Daltons make up a big group."

"It's big enough that they won't miss us."

Her eyes narrowed. "You don't want to go?"

"Not really, if that's okay with you."

Puffing out a sigh, Bliss tapped the small lid of a can marked Sea Glass back in place with a small hammer. "We can't put off seeing your family forever."

In the past two weeks alone, he had turned down an invitation to a game night and a pizza night with Wyatt and Mick. "I'm not ready to tell them about Asa, and it's not easy being around them, knowing they're my—you know."

"Your sisters. That fact won't change how they feel about you."

"It might. Remember how upsetting it was for them to learn Asa made an addendum to his will just for me? They were confused and even a bit angry, rightfully so. They'll feel both of those things again, and more, when they learn Asa cheated on their mom."

"I think they are already quite familiar with their dad's history."

"Can you imagine how Natalie will feel, being just a few months older than I am? I don't want to hurt her that way. Or Sadie or Dove."

"I know. But none of that is your fault." She gave his arm a friendly pat. "And we can't keep avoiding them. Sadie helped me set up a fundraiser for the Easter baskets at church. Little cacti in cute eggshell planters. Anyway, she just texted. Your cousins want to help pack up the baskets—next weekend because Dove has something going this weekend."

They weren't his cousins. "I don't think we need any assistance."

"No, but that's not the point." Her lips stretched into a soft smile. "I know this is hard, but they love you, and you love them. This will work out. How could it not? You've got a big heart, Thatcher."

"Not as big as Juniper's." At Bliss's questioning expression, he exhaled the stress of the conversation about his family, glad to change the topic. "That's what I came here to tell you. She asked me a question this morning. I want to say yes, but we need to talk about it first."

Her smile spread a fraction wider. "Is it about getting a cat?"

"Cat? That's fine, but no. It's about calling us Mom and Dad once the adoption is final."

Bliss's smile melted like hot wax. "Mom and Dad?"

He nodded and her eyes filled with tears.

He had literally just told himself there would be no more hugging, but maybe just this once more. He held out his arms.

"I've always wanted to be called Mom." Her breath was hot against his shirt. "I can't imagine life without Juniper, but she had a mom already. I respect that, so I never expected—"

She started crying in earnest.

He let her dampen the front of his flannel shirt. She was warm and soft, smelling of paint and coffee. He rested his chin atop the crown of her head. "I know, Bliss. These are happy tears."

She sniffled and took a ragged breath. "Very happy." She inched back, out of his hold, digging into her front jeans pocket. Tugging out a folded tissue, she blotted her eyes and cheeks. "What do you think?"

"It's not something I expected to be called, either. I know we haven't been married long, but I'm committed to Juniper, and if she wants to do this, I say yes."

Bliss's eyes filled with tears again, but she blinked them back and smiled. "I also say yes to the cat. Especially for a little girl who has made a lot of wishes, and not all of them will come true. I didn't tell you she wants a sibling."

Thatcher's stomach cinched. "Yeah, we can get the cat."

He'd made so few promises in his life, but in the past month, he had promised to care for Juniper the rest of his life, and to love, honor and cherish Bliss. He would love

Bliss, all right, but as the best friend he could possibly be. No matter how much he cared for her, or yearned to make her laugh or hold her in his arms again.

He had promised a friendship, nothing more. And he couldn't risk messing things up when he had promised her the stability and peace she deserved.

Chapter Eight

"Where do you want these?"

Just over a week later, Bliss looked up from tugging on the cranking mechanism of the casement window. The church conference room smelled like old pizza, lingering evidence that the youth group had last used the space when they'd rehearsed for an Easter play. Nothing a little fresh air wouldn't fix.

Sweet air trickled through the window now, but once Bliss turned around, the air seemed to leave her lungs. Thatcher waited inside the doorway, his well-muscled arms laden with canvas shopping bags, and his chocolate-rich gaze on Bliss. And sometimes, when he looked at her like that, she had trouble thinking.

How ridiculous. What did it say about her that mere eye contact with a man made her brain fog up?

It's not just a man, you goose. Only Thatcher has that effect on you.

"Anywhere on the table, thanks." Ugh, she sounded hoarse.

Thatcher's brows knit. "I hope your allergies aren't bothering you."

"I'm just a little scattered. I broke a water pitcher in the kitchen."

She had come in early to reset the room so she and

Thatcher's family could pack up the Easter baskets. Thatcher was still uneasy about hanging out with his family, but in the week since he and Bliss discussed it at the ranch house, he'd admitted he couldn't avoid them forever.

So, this morning, he had packed up his truck with the items Bliss ordered for the baskets, and she'd gone ahead to church to set things up, leaving Thatcher and Juniper to follow. Speaking of her foster daughter… "Where's Juniper?"

"Patting Gidget." He pulled packages of jelly beans from one of the bags. "Dutch and Beatie just arrived."

"I didn't realize they'd be here to help. They're the sweetest people. Did you remind her to come inside with them, though?"

"No, but I'm sure she knows to." Thatcher dropped the packages and strode toward her. "If she doesn't, I'll call her in, myself, but she's safe, Bliss."

"I worry when Juniper doesn't have any adults within earshot. I can't help it."

He lifted her chin with his work-rough fingers, so she had no choice but to look up at him. "She hasn't had a seizure since Dr. Cruz adjusted her medication. And that doesn't mean she'll never have one again, but God's got her. Trust Him."

Easier said than done, when it came to her foster daughter.

Help my weak faith, Lord.

Before she finished her prayer, Natalie and Pastor Luke entered the room, each carrying a box that Thatcher had packed in his truck. Thatcher's hand fell and he hurried toward them. "Let me get that for you, Nat."

"It's not heavy. Must be nothing but Easter grass in this one."

Pastor Luke set down his box. "Thanks for resetting the table and chairs, Bliss. I completely forgot to do that for you. It's been busier than usual around here since Edna took sick leave."

The parish secretary's bout of viral pneumonia had lasted almost a month now. "Could Edna use one of these baskets?"

"Oh, she'd love it, I'm sure. She's much better, but moving slowly. This experience has got her thinking it's time to retire. Wilbur has been eager to putter around the country in their RV."

Natalie unpacked packages of Easter grass from her box. "We'll miss her around here, but we understand."

"I miss her already, not just as a friend, but as a coworker. I'm buried under paperwork and bills, and I can't make heads or tails of the books."

"Financial books, you mean?" Bliss looked up from stacking Easter baskets.

Pastor Luke adjusted his glasses farther up his nose. "Exactly."

"I'm a certified bookkeeper. I'm happy to take a look at everything while Juniper is at school, if you'd like."

"That would be marvelous, but I hate to impose on you while you're job hunting."

She shook her head. "My résumé is still out at a few places, but for the most part I've taken a break from searching to fix up the ranch house. We just moved in yesterday."

"You made it look like a real home," Thatcher added. "I love it already."

After never receiving praise from the men in her life, Bliss didn't take his words for granted. She flashed him a smile, which Pastor Luke didn't miss, judging by the pleased expression on his face.

"I know you've been busy since the wedding," he said, "but I'd love to chat with you two. It's not too late for premarital counseling, but at the very least, I'd love to send you home with a copy of the book I use."

"We haven't forgotten your offer. I'm sorry it's been so busy, but for now, the book would be great," Thatcher said on his way out the door to grab another load from the car.

It didn't feel great to Bliss, though. Why didn't she want to read the book? Because her marriage wasn't real? Or was she ashamed to tell Pastor Luke the truth about their marriage?

Lane's voice rarely came into her head anymore, but she heard it now. *It's none of the preacher's business.*

That voice used to make her bow her head in humiliation, but no more. She refused to listen, but at the same time, she would have to pray about her hesitation to be transparent with Pastor Luke.

She needed God's wisdom. In the meantime, Natalie started emptying another box. Thatcher reentered the room with more bags, followed by Dove and Sadie.

Pastor Luke examined the piles atop the table. "Look at all the things you managed to find. And on such a tight budget, too."

"Sadie helped me fundraise by selling these at the farmstand." Bliss gestured at the box Sadie set down, full of tiny rose cacti planted in pastel pots that looked like Easter eggs. "We ordered extra to share in the baskets. They're seasonal and fun, but don't require much attention."

"Just my speed," the pastor joked.

Dutch, Beatie and Juniper came in then, with both Gidget and Coco wearing serene expressions and their service vests. The room was full of conversation and enthusiasm, so there was no time like the present to harvest it.

"Thanks for coming, everyone." Bliss raised her voice. "With so many hands, we should have these done in a snap."

She set out the sample basket she and Sadie had crafted to serve as an example to the others, and then organized piles of each item to include.

First, the festive paper grass to cushion the basket. Next, the bundled lap blankets, then a cross suncatcher to hang in a window with the attached suction cup. After that, there was room for a slender Easter devotional, a word search puzzle book, cozy socks, unscented hand cream, dried soup mix, jelly beans, chocolate rabbits, an Easter ducky plushie and the cactus wedged on top.

Last but not least, they added an Easter greeting card with the Resurrection message inside, as well as a video link for those unable to attend services in person.

They got to work, and it wasn't long before Bliss tied a final yellow bow on the last basket. Amid the mess of ribbon scraps, stray grass, shopping tags and a few errant jelly beans, the packed baskets sat atop the tables in their pastel glory, waiting for homes.

"They look marvelous." Pastor Luke rubbed his hands together. "The visitation team will drop them off to home-bound folks in the community during Holy Week. I'm certain they will bring joy to a lot of people."

"Thank you all for your help." Bliss's hands went to her heart as she surveyed their friends and family once again. "This went so much faster with you pitching in."

"Cleanup will go quickly with all of us, too." Dove scooped up some discarded ribbon.

"Bliss?" Juniper gathered the hot-pink dog leash from the table. "I think Coco needs out. I know where to go."

"We'll go with you." Beatie tipped her head at Dutch. "Gidget could use a break, too."

"Thanks for going with her," she whispered to Beatie as she passed.

Beatie winked, and Dutch gave her a smile. "We'll keep an eye on her."

"Want to pick a date to have dinner or brunch together?" Natalie nested the empty boxes. "You guys have been so busy lately we've hardly seen you."

Bliss forced herself not to look at Thatcher. His avoidance of his family had clearly been noted.

"Sorry about that." Thatcher scratched the back of his neck. "Fixing up the ranch house has been our top priority. Plus, the break in the north fence caused a bit of trouble, especially with reports of coyotes and a mountain lion in the area."

Natalie frowned. "Have you accounted for all of your cattle?"

"Yeah." Thatcher rubbed his eyes. "Thankfully."

"You'll have to visit our new place once we're all tidy." Bliss tried to change the subject. "There are still boxes everywhere."

"We don't care about that," Sadie said. "But I get it. You've had a lot on your plate lately."

"It'll settle down soon." Thatcher hooked his thumb at the doorway. "I'm going to grab the vacuum cleaner."

His departure seemed abrupt to Bliss, but hopefully the Dalton sisters didn't notice. But then she remembered something. "I moved the vacuum to the kitchen. He'll never find it there. Be right back." She slipped out after him, waiting until he was all the way down the hall before she called his name in a stage whisper.

He turned on his bootheel. "Everything okay?"

"The vacuum isn't in the janitorial closet—I left it in the kitchen. But while I get it, maybe you should go talk to your cousins. This is hanging over you like a dark cloud."

He rubbed his hairline as if the thoughts behind it pained

him. "I know what you're saying, but I should talk to my mom first."

"Fair enough." Doreen would be able to provide valuable insight. "But you can't let this go on forever. When is she coming home from her cruise?"

"Monday, I think, but I want to let her settle back in before I drop this big of a bomb on her."

"I'm sure she'll appreciate a few days to get over her jet lag."

They still whispered, standing close together in the hall. Bliss suddenly grew aware of just how close. His breadth filled the hall, and the air was laced with his soap and shaving cream. If she took half a step forward, she could rest against his chest, and feel comforted by his strong, warm arms—

Meanwhile, they had a group of people waiting on them. And this kind of thinking wasn't just ridiculous, it was dangerous. "I'll, um, grab the vacuum," she said.

"I'll take care of that, and you check on Juniper. You'll feel better once you see she's okay."

He was right, of course. She hurried outside, where Juniper was just fine out in the sunshine with Dutch and Beatie, while Gidget grazed on the grass and Coco lay nearby. She chatted with them for a minute, and by the time Bliss returned to the conference room, everything looked much cleaner. Dove vacuumed, Natalie tidied the table and Thatcher broke down the smaller boxes for the recycling bin.

Bliss gathered the tray holding the water pitcher and glasses, which no one had used because they'd all brought water bottles. At least she didn't need to wash the glasses. "I'll be right back."

She took it down the hall to the church kitchen, poured

the water into the sink and wiped the pitcher dry. Then she returned it to the cupboard with the glasses. On her way back to the conference room, she could hear Juniper giggling from down the hall. She hurried to see the source of the fun.

Juniper and Coco were engaged in a game of tug-of-war with one of the leftover duck plushies. Coco's paws pranced as she pulled, and Juniper knelt before her, wiggling the duck back and forth as if threatening to yank it from Coco's mouth. "Gonna get it, girl? Huh?"

Coco deserved fun and exercise like any other dog, but she knew never to engage in it unless her vest was off, a signal that her work was done—although Coco executed her job day and night, vest or no vest. But now that Juniper had removed it, Coco understood she could relax a little, just like the adults watching their antics.

And Coco had a strong fondness for stuffed animals.

Watching Juniper and Coco play was one of Bliss's favorite things to do. They exuded pure happiness, and it made Bliss feel as if everything were right in the world, even if it was only for a moment.

Juniper released the duck and rubbed Coco with both hands. "That's a good girl. You keep the ducky now. Thatcher said we could each have one."

As Coco trotted off to the corner with her duck, Thatcher offered Juniper one of the other stuffed ducks from the table. It was a pale blue, her favorite color, and she reached out to hug him.

Thatcher was so good for Juniper, and their growing closeness was healthy, important and right. But watching them, Bliss's heart pinched a little. Loneliness had been her stalwart companion for her whole life, even when she was married, but it was different now. She had a family and a home.

But she would never have the same sort of freedom Juniper enjoyed with Thatcher. Her little girl could love him with her whole heart, freely, and he could love her back—

Why was she even thinking about Thatcher in terms of *love*? She could like him, even be drawn to him, but love? Terror filled her chest.

Lord, please nip this—whatever this feeling is—in the bud. Help me find joy in all of life's blessings, including Thatcher's heart for Juniper, and not spoil them with unacceptable feelings.

I can't get hurt again, God. I can't.

She turned around and fussed with a bow on one of the baskets so no one would see the hot tears filling her eyes.

The following Friday afternoon, Thatcher stifled a yawn as he lowered himself from the saddle. Last night's heavy rain showers had kept him awake half the night, but he was nevertheless grateful for every drop in this time of drought.

It made the land a little soggy, though. Mud splattered both him and Maverick, and the mud sucked at his boots with loud squelching sounds. He approached Frank, who sat on his haunches by the north fence line they had recently repaired.

"Is it a coyote?"

Frank, the foreman, squinted up at him. "Nope."

Thatcher bent down.

"Mountain lion." The print was unmistakable in the damp earth. The pad was less than four inches wide, so he guessed the animal who'd left it was a female. "No cub prints, though."

Frank made a grunting sound as he stood. "I ain't seen

it, nor any evidence of one catching a calf, but they're more active at night, o'course."

"I'll report it to the wildlife authorities so it's on record."

"Maybe this is what's kept the coyotes away."

"Could be." Still, Thatcher felt the need to take more precautions than they had in the past. "I've got a staff meeting soon, but after that, I'll look into livestock guard dogs."

"I thought Asa's will prohibited changes." Frank tipped up the brim of his ballcap, as if he wished to get a better view of Thatcher.

"About that." Thatcher didn't know where to start, or how much he wanted anyone outside the family to know, but Frank had been on Asa's payroll for over twenty years. He could tell him some details. "There's been a development. Turns out, Asa was willing to soften his stance on the issue after I met a requirement. My hands aren't tied so tightly anymore."

"How loose is the string, boss? Because dogs are great, but it would sure help if we could extend into the field that's just sitting there. I never understood why Asa didn't want it to be used as grazing land. It's better."

Agreed. "I need a loan first."

Thankfully, Frank didn't ask for details. He just nodded once, then scanned the fence line. "How soon do you suppose we can get some dogs out here?"

Thatcher appreciated Frank's inherent lack of nosiness. "I'll reach out to Mick. He'll help me find the best breed for the job."

"You need one that doesn't react to kids and other dogs, now that you've got those in your house."

Exactly. "In the meantime, I'll price some motion-activated lights and some other deterrents."

They discussed particulars while they checked for more

tears or signs of the mountain lion. Finding none, Thatcher sent up a prayer of thanks. Then his watch beeped, reminding him he needed to head back to make it to the farmstand office in time.

Not that he wanted to go to a staff meeting. It still felt weird being around Natalie, Sadie and Dove, although he'd managed well enough when they'd packed up the Easter baskets. Maybe because there were other people around. But it didn't help that office meetings were the least favorite part of his job. He'd far rather be out with the animals.

At least Bliss would be there, a source of comfort and peace. He had never known a friendship like this, and just thinking about her made the idea of the meeting far more tolerable.

He thumped Frank's shoulder. "I've gotta go. Catch up with you later."

"Say hi to the missus," Frank teased. "I know that's what put the spark in your eye just now."

Spark? Must have been the sun's reflection…although his eyes were shielded by the bill of his ball cap. He decided not to bite Frank's bait. "Bye, Frank."

He mounted Maverick and guided him toward home, swaying with the gelding's easy gait. The sun was warm on his shoulders, and the sweet smell of rain-damp vegetation perfumed the air—a beautiful scent after a long dry spell. There was so much to thank God for, and he'd be remiss if he didn't take a few moments to reflect on his blessings.

He was still counting the number of good things in his life while he finished caring for Maverick. Then he dropped into the ranch office, grabbed a folder off his desk, and walked the half-mile to the Foxtail Farm office behind the farmstand.

It looked like Dutch was running a minute behind, too.

He met the orchard manager at the office door. "Heading in?"

"Only to drop off my report." Dutch held a yellow sheet torn from a legal-sized pad. "Everything in the orchard is business as usual, except spider mites are going to take over the Golden Delicious and Rome Beauty orchards if we don't fight back fast. I need to handle it myself because we're a few folks short in the orchard. There's some sort of stomach bug going around."

"Juniper said some kids in her class were home with it." Thatcher hoped they avoided it. "Want me to take the report in for you?"

"That would be a big help, thanks. I won't keep you standing here, when you surely want to see that pretty wife of yours." Dutch handed over the paper. "Not that you haven't seen her all day, now that you all are living right at the ranch."

"Actually, she's been at church today, helping Pastor Luke with church accounts."

"Then go give your bride a kiss. And I'll go give one to my bride, too."

There would be no kissing Bliss, but Thatcher was nevertheless eager to see her. He strode into the office, tugging off his ball cap as he went.

Dove and Sadie were busy doctoring their coffee with sugar and creamer, and Natalie sat at the scratched table, tapping on her phone. Bliss was kitty-corner to her, with her folders and laptop ready. When she saw him, she smiled shyly.

He said hello to the room at large, but his gaze was on Bliss. As if drawn by a magnet, he walked straight to the vacant seat next to her. "How did it go at church?"

"I'll have those records untangled in another visit or two. How's the fence line?"

"Good, but I found a mountain lion track. I'd like to get some livestock guard dogs. I'll talk to Mick, but I'm thinking of Kangal Shepherd Dogs. They can handle the summer heat—"

"Did you say lion track?" Natalie looked a little pale at the thought. "It's been a while since we've had one on the property, that we know of, anyway."

Dove sat down across from Thatcher. "You're free to get guard dogs now according to Dad's addendum for you? I never did understand all the details."

There was a slight edge to her tone that made Thatcher want to get back on Maverick and ride away. He couldn't blame her curiosity, but the guilt that flared up in him was part of why he had been avoiding his family.

He decided to stick to the facts. "I'm still bound to the property like all of you. I can't move away. I can extend the border, as long as I don't infringe on the orchards, but I don't have a loan yet so…nothing is changing there. But I think I can get dogs now."

Sadie sat with a cup of milky coffee. "I know this is awkward, but we can't help wishing Dad had let us make changes, too, Thatcher."

"I wish that, too." He met Bliss's gaze again, knowing she understood how uncomfortable he was.

"Maybe we should start the meeting." Bliss shifted in her seat. "I have school pickup soon."

Sadie glanced at her watch. "But Dutch isn't here yet."

"Oh, yeah. Here's his report." Thatcher slid the yellow page across the table to Natalie. "He's battling spider mites. Otherwise, the orchard is 'the usual,' he said."

"Let's talk about the ranch, then, since we started on the subject." Natalie drew a line on her notepad. "How expensive are the dogs and the upkeep? I assume their expenses are going to come out of the existing budget for the ranch. Or is that something the loan will cover?"

"I'm not sure, yet, but I have to protect the stock."

"Let us know as soon as you find out about the loan, so we can adjust the budget. Anything else where the ranch is concerned?"

"We're still selling beef at the farmstand, but only as much as the single refrigerator case can hold." Sadie tapped her pencil. "Can we sell more now that the will has been changed, or does that not count because it would be sold at the farmstand? Dad's instructions are so confusing."

"I can ask the lawyer." Thatcher typed a note to himself on his phone.

"Shall we move on, then?" Natalie looked around.

"One last thing about the ranch." Bliss spoke up. "I wasn't aware the brand renewal fee is due by the end of April, but I found a bill. It wasn't in the budget when I started keeping Foxtail's books last year. Am I missing something?"

Thatcher searched his brain. "I completely forgot about that. I'm sorry. It's a biennial expense. That's why it was missing."

Bliss jotted a note. "Then, with your permission, I'll look into automatic payments so we don't have to worry about it again."

"That would be perfect. Wow, Bliss, I hate to think about what we'd do without you." He smiled at her.

"You've saved our bacon, Bliss. Or should I say, our beef." Natalie started to laugh, but then her eyes shut, as if she'd just remembered something.

Bliss met Thatcher's gaze, then fixed her focus on the papers. "Did I forget something that could affect the books?"

Whenever there was a hint of error or trouble, Bliss automatically assumed responsibility. Now that he knew her better, he had a better grasp of why. At least, he thought he did.

Her husband. Her father. The verbal and emotional abuse she must have suffered infuriated him. Thatcher cracked his knuckles. If he ever met Bliss's dad, he'd—

Repent of the thought he just had, and strive to handle the situation biblically, with patience and compassion, while at the same time protecting Bliss from further pain.

But in the meantime, Natalie's eyes reopened. "Sorry, nothing like that. Muscle cramp. Now, where were we?"

Bliss looked around the room. "Ready to move on to bakery sales?"

Dove leaned forward. "Not quite. I want to know more about Dad's will. Do you think we could see it?"

Thatcher's shoulders tensed. "You don't believe me?"

"That's not it. It's just so strange. And you really don't seem to want to talk about it. Since the day you told us, you've been busy, but it sure feels like you're avoiding us. I know we were all shocked about the wedding and we probably didn't seem supportive, but we tried to make up for it by throwing the reception. Are you holding a grudge?"

Bliss reached for his hand beneath the table.

Calmed instantly by her touch, he squeezed back. "No. I wish things had gone differently, but I can understand why you're upset, and we're grateful for the reception." Maybe now they could move on.

Then he flicked his hair back from his forehead. It looked cocky, he knew, but he also really needed to get his hair out of his face, and Bliss held his dominant right hand.

"Thatcher, you look just like Dad when you do that." Natalie looked at her sisters. "Doesn't he look like Dad right now?"

"It's uncanny." Dove chuckled.

Sadie made an exaggerated shrug to show she was about to tease him. "Maybe that's why Dad gave you special treatment. You look just like him, so he liked you best."

Sadie might have made it sound like a joke, but he knew there was a hard kernel of pain at its center. The women felt slighted by their dad, and he had to set at least that part of the record straight. "He didn't like me best. You know that, right?"

It was quiet for several seconds.

"He might have, for all we know." Natalie's tone was sad.

Sadie's chin quavered. "We all had such complicated relationships with our dad, and then when he died and bound us all to Foxtail, it was a blow. I mean, we all had to give up our jobs to work here. But we made do, together, all for one, one for all. But the change to Dad's will for you and you alone hurt. We're plodding along, bound by his rules, but he made your life easier."

"I wouldn't say being told I had to get married made my life easier," he blurted.

Bliss flexed her hand, as if to release his. "Maybe I should let you all talk amongst yourselves."

He gripped her hand harder. "I didn't mean it like that. Please stay. All I'm saying is that it was a bizarre thing for Asa to do."

"I know." Bliss's soft gaze told him she understood far beyond what the words he was saying. She had been his rock through the turbulence of the past month.

Dove folded her arms. "It might be childish for us to

think that Dad liked you better than his own daughters, but it crossed all of our minds, anyway. And it stinks to think that about your own dad."

Thatcher could only nod. "It does, but I assure you, he didn't lift my restrictions because he liked me better."

"Then why did he do something that favored you over his own daughters?" Natalie leaned back in her chair. "Why did he bless you and ignore us?"

He couldn't feel Bliss's hand tethering him to earth anymore. All he felt was anger. "It wasn't about blessing or favor. It was entirely about manipulating me, because when you're Asa Dalton and you think your kid is going to turn out to be as rotten as you were, you do something drastic to try to prevent that from happening, I guess—"

The breath froze halfway out his lungs. No. He'd practically said he was Asa's kid.

And quick glances at the others showed they hadn't missed it.

Dove spoke first. "*Your kid.* Asa's kid?"

"I didn't mean to say that."

Not yet. Not like this.

But he couldn't lie to them now.

He turned first to Bliss, feeling like he needed her forgiveness. "I had no choice."

"I know. This…just happened." She lifted his hand and held it to her soft cheek, anchoring him to her. Her strength. Her peace. "And it'll be okay."

He held her gaze for a full second before he turned back to meet each of his sisters in the eye, one after the other.

"I think Jake and Doreen adopted me." He hated the words coming out of his mouth. "I don't know who my biological mother is, but I'm pretty sure Asa was my father."

Natalie stared at him in horror, her face reflecting the dread swirling in his gut.

Then, covering her mouth, she bolted from the room, shoving the door open so hard it slammed behind her.

Chapter Nine

Bliss flinched at the loud smack of the office door against the frame, but she gripped Thatcher's hand. He couldn't have clung any tighter to hers had she been the only thing preventing him from falling off a cliff.

"I'll go check on her." Sadie left the room without meeting their eyes.

Bliss sent a prayer heavenward. Only God could heal the wounds ripping the Daltons apart right now.

"I made her sick." Thatcher tipped his head back.

Bliss wouldn't let him blame himself. None of this was his fault. It was Asa's. "She might be upset, understandably so, but that doesn't mean she's having a physical response to the news. It could be the stomach bug that's going around."

"Or food poisoning." Dove sounded surprisingly calm, her tone conversational. "She and I took the twins to lunch at that new bistro on Sycamore. Maybe her Shrimp Louie salad was bad."

"Did Rose and Luna eat some?" Bliss bit her lip. "I don't mean to overstep, but if they have food poisoning, they could dehydrate quickly because they're so young."

Dove waved a hand. "They had mac and cheese."

"That's good, but…" Thatcher let out a ragged sigh. "Aren't you going to yell at me or something?"

"Why would I do that?" Dove pulled a face.

"Because you probably hate my guts right now."

"That doesn't describe me. I can't guarantee Sadie and Natalie won't have a lot of questions when they come back, though."

Thatcher exchanged another look with Bliss. "I guess we should wait and see, then."

They didn't have to wait long. Natalie reentered the room on Sadie's arm, looking as limp as an overcooked noodle.

Thatcher jumped to his feet to pull out her chair. "I'm so sorry, Nat. Are you okay?"

Natalie rolled her eyes. "I'm fine. No need to fuss."

"It's okay if you're *not* fine." Bliss hopped up to get a bottle of water from the minifridge by the coffee maker. "You've had a shock."

"You might want to go home," Dove added, "in case the shrimp isn't through with you yet."

"Or you caught the flu." Thatcher looked like a dejected dog, staring at Natalie as if he wished she'd look at him. "If you're too weak, I can carry you to my truck and drive you."

"It's not the flu." Natalie rubbed her neck. "Or the shrimp."

"Then it's me."

"It's not you, either, Thatcher. It's—well, maybe this was how you felt five minutes ago, not wanting to say something, but the cat is halfway out of the bag now, so... I have an announcement." In a weary gesture, Natalie rubbed the curved shadow beneath her right eye. "Wyatt and I are expecting a baby in October."

It was quiet for a full second. Then Thatcher groaned. "Oh, Nat. I never would have told you about Asa if I'd known you're pregnant. What if I hurt you or the baby by dropping that bomb on you?"

"I have morning sickness, you goose. To be honest, though, it's 'all-day sickness' right now. I've been throwing up all day. Although your news was a big shock."

"First things first." Sadie circled her sister in a hug. "Congratulations are in order."

"They sure are. A new baby!" Dove joined in the sisterly embrace.

Bliss and Thatcher held back. Maybe he didn't want to join because his recent announcement lingered in the room, heavy and dark. And he, like her, wasn't quite sure if his touch would be welcome just yet.

But Bliss's joy and smile for her friends were real. "How wonderful. I'm so happy for you and Wyatt, Natalie."

"Me, too. Congratulations." Thatcher's arm went around Bliss's shoulders, as if he understood the news about a baby might be bittersweet to her. And it was. As happy as she was for her friends, she was the teeniest bit sad because of her miscarriages.

But this wasn't the time for self-pity or regret. They had a new life to celebrate. She hoped her smile communicated to Thatcher that she was okay. He seemed to understand, because he lowered his arm.

The sisters broke apart, and then, looking at Thatcher and Bliss, their smiles faltered a bit.

But they didn't look away, and Natalie swiped a single tear from her cheek. "Thank you. We're thrilled to expand our family. Rose and Luna will be the best big sisters."

"They will, but speaking of sisters?" Dove resumed her seat. "Do you want to talk about Thatcher's announcement now, Nat, or wait until you feel better?"

"Wait," Thatcher spoke before Natalie could. "I hate that I made you sick—and I know you said that I didn't, but I blame myself anyway. I don't want to hurt you or the baby."

"If we don't talk about this now, I'll stew over questions. And either way, I'll have morning sickness. It's okay, Thatcher. Why don't you start at the beginning? Tell us why you believe you're our br—brother."

Bliss prayed for him, even though her heart felt ripped in half.

Thatcher stared at the table. "Bliss found some boxes in the ranch house packed with memorabilia from my childhood, accompanied by notes from Doreen to Asa." Then he explained about the blood types and Rh factors.

"So you think you're Asa's because of blood types and boxes of report cards?" Sadie scratched her fingernail atop the table.

"You don't think that's compelling evidence? Because I do." Dove turned to Thatcher. "I believed you the instant it came out of your mouth. It explains a lot, like why Dad wanted you here every summer."

"And why he gave you the ranch," Natalie added. "To make up for not being a dad to you."

"But he knew I'd be the first one of us to grow restless." Thatcher toed his boot into the linoleum. "So he forced me to do what he wanted or I'd lose the ranch, plain and simple."

"I hope that's not why he did it." Sadie sounded exhausted. "I wish he had been honest with us before he died. About everything."

"Our dad was a piece of work." Dove jumped up and wrapped her arms around Thatcher. "We love you."

"We sure do." Sadie's eyes were damp. "And this isn't your fault."

"We're family." Natalie nodded, but her cheeks were pale. "But let's not say anything to Mom until Aunt Doreen has confirmed this. Is that okay?"

"Completely." There was hope in Thatcher's expression.

Bliss could've cried in relief and gratitude. It would have to wait, though, because her phone started buzzing. A shiver of panic raced through her, as it always did when her phone lit up like this. She always wondered if Juniper was okay.

But thankfully, it wasn't the school. It was Juniper's grandma, Vera. She would have to return the call later, but she also saw a text on the screen from Pastor Luke.

"Everything okay?" Thatcher looked at her over Dove's shoulder.

"Pastor Luke can't get into the accounting software, which is weird, because I didn't log him out. Hopefully it's a quick fix because I need to pick up Juniper from school."

"Go do what you need to do. I can get Juniper."

"She has a dental appointment right after school, though."

"I can take her. Frank and the guys have everything under control at the ranch, and I can do a little work on my phone while I'm in the waiting room during her appointment. It's Dr. Peck, right?"

A tiny voice that sounded like Olivia's reminded her that others didn't find Thatcher to be trustworthy, but she shut the voice down. He had proven himself to be reliable countless times.

"Right." She gathered her purse. "Before you go into Dr. Peck's, Coco might need a little break."

"Got it. Meet you at home?"

"Perfect." Bliss packed her work bag. "Congratulations again, Natalie," she said as she left.

The staff meeting had not gone as planned, but there was relief in knowing the truth was out, at least to the people who were most affected by it. Maybe it was good Bliss was leaving the siblings alone to talk, too.

Praying for them, she drove back to the white church and parked on the street, just outside the red door. She walked around the side of the building to the office. Poor Pastor Luke's hair stood on end on the sides, as if he'd been pulling at it.

"I'm sorry to call you back here."

"Not a problem at all. Let's see if we can figure this out."

Bliss took his place at the computer, and sure enough, the accounting program was unresponsive. She messed with it for a while to no avail before turning to Pastor Luke. "I'm at a loss. The only thing I can think to try is rebooting the computer."

"Let's give it a shot."

She manually turned the machine off. "We need to give it a minute."

"If that's all it takes, I apologize bringing you back just for this."

"I don't mind. Thatcher is picking up Juniper so I have plenty of time."

"I always suspected Thatcher would make a good dad, and not just because he's so good with Natalie and Wyatt's twins. He's patient and humble. Not a lot of people see that side of him, but you obviously did, since you married him."

"He's a good man. Otherwise I wouldn't have said yes. I only want what's best for Juniper." Even if it meant marrying a man she hadn't loved.

Couldn't love, then or now—

Stop thinking in terms of love. Partnership, yes. For Juniper and the ranch.

But maybe their relationship needed something more than friendship to hold it together. They may not share romantic love, but shouldn't they build their home on the firm foundation of Christ?

"I think it's safe to turn this on again." Bliss pushed the button. It was silent for a moment, and then the computer whirred to life. "While it loads, could I bother you for a copy of the book on marriage you told us about?"

"I'll fetch it. One moment."

By the time Pastor Luke returned, she had logged back into the accounting program. "It was a glitch, and all it took was the reboot—ah, thank you." She accepted the bright blue paperback and tucked it into her purse. As she did so, she could hear her phone buzzing.

Vera again. "I'm sorry, but this is Juniper's grandma. It's the second time she had reached out today, so I'd better take it."

"Please. Thanks for coming by to help. Twice. What would I do without you?"

"My pleasure." Truly. She enjoyed the calm, friendly atmosphere in the office, and the brief conversations she'd had today with Pastor Luke as well as Karis, the church preschool director. "I'll be back tomorrow to work on the books."

She answered the call on the way out the door. "Hi, Vera. How are you?"

"I'm upright," she joked.

"I'm sorry I haven't yet responded to your earlier call, but I was in a meeting. Is everything okay?"

"I have news." Her words came out slowly, which set Bliss's heart racing.

Was she worse? Or was Juniper's dad out of jail and wanting her back? If so, that was not going to be easy, because he'd signed away his rights, and—

Bliss stopped the panicky train of her thoughts. *Lord,*

help me not get ahead of myself. Vera sometimes liked to build up tension and drama, and this could be one of those times. "What is it?"

"I was talking to Ramona. You remember her? From three doors down?"

"Yes." Not vividly, but if Vera's neighbor at the assisted living facility was involved in this story, then the news probably didn't have to do with Juniper's dad or Vera being sicker. She sent up a prayer of gratitude as she unlocked her car door.

"Her nephew visited today. Very handsome boy. He and Ramona stopped in to get me for lunch, and he saw your photo on my coffee table. 'I know her,' he said. Sterling Branden-something."

"Brandenburg?" Bliss sat behind the wheel. "What a small world. We were in school together. He and his wife were lovely people." Her only friends at one point.

"He's starting a bookkeeping business just a few miles down from here, and he's looking to hire good people. I told him how you've been looking for work for weeks now and that you're adopting my granddaughter, and that you're the most trustworthy person in the world."

Vera's words warmed Bliss's heart. "That's so sweet of you, Vera. As long as I live, I will never get over the incredible honor of raising your granddaughter. Thank you for trusting me. As for Sterling, I'm happy to reconnect with him, but I can't take a job in San Diego." Making that hour-plus commute daily didn't sound appealing. Not when those valuable minutes could be spent with Juniper.

Besides, she didn't need a job as desperately now that she was married.

"You wouldn't commute, silly. You'd move here and then I'd get to see my Juniper every day."

All the warm fuzzy feelings evaporated like dew beneath a scorching summer sun. “I’m sorry, Vera. I know how much you and Juniper miss each other, but she and I can’t move right now. Thatcher is bound to his ranch.”

It was quiet a full five seconds. “Who’s Thatcher?”

Oh, no. Bliss prayed for wisdom. “My husband, Vera. I got married in February.”

The silence stretched. Then Vera made a sound with her tongue. “The big fellow who gave me chocolate.”

“Yes. It was Valentine’s Day.” Bliss’s chest ached.

“He was a hunk, as I recall.”

Funny that Vera remembered *that.* “You’re not wrong.”

“It slipped my mind. But I didn’t forget about Sterling Branden-Bergdorf, though. He said he would call you next week. Let me look at my calendar so I can tell you what those days are.”

“It’s okay, I don’t need the dates—”

“Oh, that’s Juniper’s birthday. I can’t believe she’ll be seven already. Is it all right if I send you money to buy her a new doll from me?”

Juniper wouldn’t be seven. She’d be ten.

Occasional memory lapses were normal. Bliss had her fair share, but something more could be off with Vera today. It was a lot to process when Bliss’s thoughts and emotions were already in a whirlwind over Thatcher telling his cousins he was actually their brother. It was starting to feel like Bliss had been on a roller coaster too long and it was time to stop the ride.

“Sure, Vera. We can talk more about it later, if you like.”

“Yes, maybe after my nap.”

After disconnecting the call, Bliss dialed the assisted living facility and spoke to a manager. The woman promised to monitor Vera and leave a message for her doctor, but reminded her that the stroke had affected Vera's memory. And since Bliss did not have power of attorney, she could not legally get involved.

Her shoulders heavy, Bliss started the car and drove home, unsure how to pray beyond asking God to help. By the time she pulled into Foxtail Ranch, her burdens were just as weighty, but she could sense God's peace.

She drove past the office to the little house, where she parked beneath the scrub oaks next to Thatcher's truck. Juniper waved from the swing Thatcher had strung up for her, pumping her legs to go higher in the air while Coco rested on the grass below, her pink tongue lolling out in contentment. The front door was propped open, allowing the breeze into the house through the new screen door, and a shadow of movement told her Thatcher was just inside.

The scene was so sweet and bucolic that she was overcome by a sense of homecoming. She let out a sigh.

"Hi, baby," Bliss called once she got out of the car.

Thatcher appeared on the porch. "Welcome home."

"Thanks." It felt good to be able to relax now, after such a long and emotionally-draining day. "How was the dentist?"

"What dentist?" Juniper pumped higher on the swing.

Thatcher scrubbed his face with his hands. "Oh, Bliss. I'm so sorry. On the way to pick up Juniper I heard the loan was denied. But it's no excuse. I blew it."

The loan was denied? Everest Sloane had made this personal, no question.

"These things happen, Thatcher. We'll reschedule." Her voice sounded a little more resigned than she had intended it to, but she blamed it on fatigue.

"I'm sorry we forgot the dentist." Juniper didn't sound

the least bit disappointed. "But I got 95% on my spelling test."

"Way to go. You studied hard. How about we order a pizza for dinner?"

"Hawaiian-style?"

"With extra pineapple." She glanced at Thatcher as she walked past him up the porch, registering his unhappy expression. "Are you upset about the dentist? It's all right."

"It's not all right that I forgot. I'm just like *him*."

She knew who he meant. Asa.

"Come inside, please." She didn't want to have a discussion like this within Juniper's hearing.

Thatcher wanted to kick himself into next week. "I'm so sorry, Bliss. I was at school in the pickup line to get Juniper, and I checked email on my phone. I saw the loan was denied and her dentist appointment flew right out of my head."

"I can't blame you for being distracted." She set down her bags on the floor inside the door. "What a disappointment about the loan."

"What's disappointing is that I forgot about everything but my selfish problems." And he needed to take full responsibility for it, as well as for his actions. "I'll call Dr. Peck's office and apologize. I'll reschedule and I'll be the one to take her. And if there's a fee for missing the appointment, I'll cover it."

"I don't think there's a fee, and you don't need to take her. You have a full-time job, but I'm home."

He didn't feel any better about his thoughtlessness, but she looked so tired, he set it aside for the moment. "Come here." He strode into the kitchen. He pulled a glass down from the cupboard and filled it with ice and water. She stood behind him, and he offered it to her. "How did it go with the computer at church?"

"It was frozen and I had to reboot. No big deal, but then Vera called. She forgot I was married and told me about a bookkeeping job in San Diego."

"Uh-oh." He knew she wouldn't move away, but the thought of it still made him edgy.

Bliss leaned against the counter. "She also forgot Juniper's age, so after we hung up, I called the assisted living office. They said they'd keep an eye on her, but it's hard for me not to be concerned."

"I'm sorry. That's rough."

"I'll have to take Juniper for a visit soon. We've been so busy I haven't taken her since the wedding." She took a sip of water. "It's been a rough day all around. How did it go at Foxtail after I left?"

"Stilted. I know they care about me, but I don't think any of us know how we're supposed to act."

"It will be awkward for a while, but you'll all adjust. You're their family."

"I was their family when I was their cousin, if that makes sense, but now that I'm their brother? That might be too painful for them to ever accept."

"You didn't do this, though. Asa did."

He caught his distorted reflection in the silvery sink tap. Nothing about him looked right in the shiny chrome, but he could make out his eyes perfectly. Eyes that looked so much like Asa's.

It was time to admit it aloud. "There's more than Asa's blood running through me, Bliss. I've got his good intentions, just like he did, but also the same inability to make good on them."

"That's not true at all."

"Isn't it? He cared, otherwise he wouldn't have kept all of those mementos. He brought me here every summer. I care about Juniper, but I messed up today, the same way he always did. He 'forgot' important things all the time."

"There's a difference between forgetting a dental appointment and her birthday, the way he forgot yours, Thatcher."

She remembered the story? That memory still made him feel like a puppy left in a box labeled Free outside the supermarket.

And he never wanted Juniper to feel that way because of him. "Asa was ultimately incapable of being a good dad, and it looks like I could be that way, too."

"One mistake with the dentist—"

"There will be more mistakes. I'll hurt both you and Juniper."

"What are you saying?" Her eyes grew wide, as if she were frightened he would leave. Shouldn't she be more frightened of being stuck with him?

"All I'm saying is I'm sorry. I'm clearly wired to be selfish."

"Yeah." Her voice was strong. "You are."

He had expected her to argue with him, but instead, she stared him down.

"I'm selfish, too, Thatcher. It's called being human, but I thought you and I believed in the same God. The One who changes lives. Jesus didn't leave me the way He found me. You're not the same person you used to be, either, yet here you are, discounting everything He has done in you and for you."

"I—I have a long way to go, that's all. And I wouldn't blame you if—"

"Shh."

"What?"

"I heard something."

"It's my phone." He tugged it from his pocket. "Mom. We've been playing phone tag since she got back from the cruise, but it can wait."

"That wasn't it." She brushed past him, her head angled like Coco's when a chipmunk skittered nearby. "It was a thump, like the screen door shutting." She dashed into the living room, pushed the screen door and stepped onto the porch. "Juniper?"

He looked straight over Bliss's head. The swing was still, as if no one had been on it for the past minute or so.

"Juniper?" Bliss called, hurrying down the porch steps.

"She's okay, Bliss."

"How can she be okay if she was eavesdropping and heard us talk like that? She must be so upset that she ran off."

"She knows to ask permission before going anywhere."

"That wouldn't stop her from running off if she's crying."

Something occurred to him, and every drop of blood in Thatcher's body seemed to sink to his feet. There was a mountain lion in the area. An attack was unlikely, but he would never risk Juniper's life on a probability.

"We've got to find her." He took off running, praying she was safe.

Chapter Ten

Panic clawed at Bliss's throat. *God, please keep Juniper safe. Please.*

She should trust Him, but her brain and body no longer seemed to understand the word. Her heart pounded adrenaline through her as she raced behind Thatcher.

They checked the barn and office. Empty. Juniper wasn't at the fence, at least as far down the line as they could see.

Any other nine-year-old could wander out of their parents' sight and it would be okay. But not Juniper, and not after she'd overheard them arguing, with Thatcher saying he didn't think he could be a good dad. Or that he would make mistakes and hurt them.

Juniper had wished for a mom and a dad, and she was probably terrified that their home would be torn apart.

Bliss cupped her hands around her mouth. "Juniper!"

Her shout bounced off the barn's brown siding in a lonely echo. Would it reach Juniper's ears? Would she respond, or be silent, wanting time alone to cry?

"Bliss." Thatcher had gone the opposite direction to look toward Foxtail Farm and the road. But he wasn't scanning the horizon now. Instead, he crouched low to the ground, his fingers tracing something in the soft earth.

She rushed toward him and looked down. The tracks of Juniper's size 3 tennis shoes led into the oaks.

"These could be old prints."

"Not with the rain we had. And when we got home today, she had a snack and then went straight out to the swing—she never walked over here. These are fresh, and it looks like she was running. There's too much growth beneath the trees for her to have left any tracks we can follow, but she'll be easy to spot once we get to the clearing. Let's take turns calling her name, and then wait a few seconds to listen for her in case she yells back. But don't tiptoe or anything. We want to be as noisy as possible."

So Juniper could hear them coming?

Oh—no, so wildlife could.

"You're worried about the mountain lion. But it's broad daylight." Still, fear caused her stomach to threaten revolt. She covered her mouth to hold back a retch.

Thatcher stopped and cupped her neck in his large hand. "Look at me, Bliss. You're right, it's plenty light right now, and she has Coco with her, but we're being smart, scaring off any critters that might be around." He turned away and took a full breath. "Juniper!"

Bliss swallowed down her fear. *Lord, protect her.* "Should we call someone for help?"

"Not yet. She can't have gone far."

Out of her sight was too far, to Bliss's thinking. "Juniper!"

They reached the old split rail fence that divided the house's lot from the fields. Thatcher braced his palms on the highest plank and leaped over. Splinters pierced her hands as she climbed atop the low rail, but then his large hands spanned her waist and he lifted her the rest of the way over.

He set her down and she trotted behind him, her stride

far shorter than his. Her gaze scanned high and low, listening in between their shouts, but all she could hear was the swish of grass and the occasional lowing of a Black Angus.

"Junebug?" Thatcher ducked to peer beneath a low-branched oak. "We're sorry, honey. Please come back. No need to hide." He turned back to Bliss. "But I can't blame her."

If anyone was to blame, it was Bliss. She should have waited until Juniper was asleep to talk seriously with Thatcher. And she probably should have waited on God's provision for a new job, rather than jump at Thatcher's proposal because it offered a quick solution for both of their problems—

Bliss shook off the negative thoughts. There would be time to examine her actions later, but right now, all they needed to do was locate Juniper, safe and sound.

Lord, please guard her.

Soon they would be out of the trees, into the open pasture. Juniper should be easy to spot in her pink sweatshirt. Bliss's pulse quickened with hope.

"Juniper?" Thatcher's shout overlapped with an all-too familiar *woof.*

"Coco!" The barks led Bliss and Thatcher to take a sharp right. They were a gift, guiding them to Juniper, but Coco was trained to bark when Juniper was seizing, and the prospect filled Bliss with fear. *Oh, Lord, how Juniper needs You now. How we need You.*

There she was, on the ground, half hidden behind a tree. Seizing.

Thatcher was far faster than Bliss. He dropped to Juniper's side, then met Bliss's gaze as she caught up to him.

"We need an ambulance."

Bliss's fingers shook so hard that she struggled to push the buttons on her phone.

* * *

A few hours later, Thatcher balanced on a hard plastic chair, watching Juniper sleep on the narrow bed in the ER cubicle. There was only room for one parent or guardian, so naturally Bliss had stayed with Juniper until now, keeping him posted while he and Coco sat in the waiting room. But Bliss hadn't had a break since they left Foxtail Ranch, so a few minutes ago, she had reluctantly agreed to trade places with him so she could stretch her legs, and she'd taken Coco with her.

Lord, thank You that Juniper's scan came back clear. Thank You that she didn't hurt her head when she fell.

His phone buzzed. It was a message from his mom.

You did the right thing, taking Jumper to the hospital.

Despite the anguish lapping at his insides, his lips twitched at the unfortunate autocorrect in his mom's text.

Thanks, Mama.

He hadn't called her that in years, not since he was a little boy. But right now, he felt as lost and alone as he had when Asa had forgotten his birthday.

Please text when you get back home, but I warn you, I might be asleep. The jetlag is REAL. Holding you all in my heart.

He tapped out a brief response, then updated his family on their group chat, as well as Frank, Dutch and Beatie, and Pastor Luke. As soon as he was finished, Juniper shifted in bed and then her eyes fluttered open.

He shoved his phone back in his pocket and took her hand in both of his. "Hey, Junebug."

"Hey. Where's Bliss?"

"She took Coco for a walk. I'm glad to have a minute with you alone, though, to tell you how sorry I am. Did you hear me and Bliss talking?"

"You said you can't be a good dad." She plucked at the coarse white blanket draped over her tiny frame. "Does that mean you're not going to be my dad anymore?"

"No. I will always be here." His stomach clenched as if he'd been punched. "It's just that my dad wasn't around much, so I don't always know what to do when it comes to being a parent. But I *want* to know, because I want to be the best dad in the world for you. Even if I make mistakes."

"Everyone makes mistakes."

"That's what Bliss said."

"So does my Sunday school teacher. She said only Jesus is perfect."

"Smart lady." He chuckled. "You're my little girl. I love you, and I'm going to stick by you forever."

Her eyes brightened. "I love you, too, Thatcher. But what about Bliss? Do you love her?"

With a loud jangle, the cubicle curtain opened, revealing a bald, fiftysomething man in a white coat, with Bliss and Coco behind him.

"Hi Juniper." The man's wide smile had a comforting quality. "I'm Dr. Kowalski. We met earlier."

"I remember." She scooched up in bed.

"Thank you for waiting so patiently while I had a video chat with your epileptologist, as well as the neurologist here at the hospital. I'm glad to report we're all on the same page. Dr. Cruz is making a small tweak to your medication, and she said she'll call Bliss tomorrow to check on you. Now, before you go, do you have any questions for me?"

Juniper shook her head.

The doctor turned to Bliss. "You can help her get ready to go home. Someone will come to escort her outside in a wheelchair. Hospital policy."

"I'll leave you to it, ladies." Thatcher followed the physician out into the hallway. "Doctor? I have a question, if you don't mind."

"Not at all." As busy as the man must be, he bore a patient expression.

"Could stress have triggered the seizure?"

The doctor's appearance turned thoughtful. "It's possible, but sometimes they just happen for reasons unknown to us. Why?"

"I was frustrated." Shame roiled in Thatcher's gut. "She overheard Bliss and I talking."

"Your wife told me about your misunderstanding. It's clear to me that Juniper is in a safe, loving environment, but none of us are immune from stress. I suggest you find a constructive way to deal with any stressors—and then model those to Juniper."

"Thank you, Doctor." His words were helpful, but Thatcher still took this experience as a warning. He never again wanted Juniper to suffer the consequences of his failures.

You know better than anyone how far I am from perfect, God, but I know You're a God of second chances and forgiveness. I'm so sorry for my thoughtlessness and selfishness. I want to be a good dad to Juniper.

I want to be more like You.

Patient. Loving. Trustworthy.

Bliss poked her head out of the cubicle. "She's ready. Just waiting for the IV to come out, and then for the wheelchair. Do you want to move the truck to the patient loading zone in front of the hospital? That way you'll be ready as soon as we come out."

"Good idea. I had to park at the opposite end of the lot, and I'd hate to make you wait outside in the cold for me." Thatcher ducked in to kiss Juniper atop the head and scratch Coco behind the ears. He wished he could give Bliss some sort of comforting gesture, but she might not even want one from him. "I'll see you out front."

He returned to the hallway, nodded at the nurse slipping in to Juniper's cubicle behind him and strode into the waiting room, tugging his keys from his front pocket.

He drew up short seeing a group sitting in a cluster near the ER's automatic doors. Mick and Sadie sat together, facing Dove, Wyatt and Natalie. "What are you all doing here?"

"Checking on you." Dove hopped up and wrapped her arms around him in a fierce hug.

"I thought you received the latest news. Juniper is fine." He had told them where they were and sent updates over the past few hours.

Mick clapped his shoulder. "We got your texts, but we wanted to support you in person."

"You mean I've been texting you from the other room, and you were here all along?"

Natalie shook her head. "We just sat down."

"Mom and Dad couldn't come sit with Rose and Luna until seven, and Mick had a vet emergency to take care of. Dove got stuck with an order—but we're all here now." Wyatt reached and pulled Thatcher into a hug. "Glad Juniper's okay."

"I was just going to text and let you know we were here. I wondered if you'd eaten, and if not, we could grab you something from the cafeteria." Sadie held up her phone. "But if you're on your way out, maybe you'd prefer to eat in the car so you can get home quicker. Mick and I can pick up something. There's a specialty market still open across the street, and they sell sandwiches. Is that okay?"

"That would be great, thanks." He would wolf it down before he drove. Juniper would probably sleep on the journey home, but Bliss could eat at her leisure. Thankfully, they had extra rations of Coco's food in the backpack. "I need to bring the truck around. We're just waiting on a wheelchair for Juniper."

"We'll hurry then." Mick grabbed Sadie's hand, and they rushed outside.

Wyatt exchanged a knowing look with Natalie before turning back to Thatcher. "Why don't we go with you to get the truck?"

"And I'll wait here for Bliss and Juniper," Dove announced.

Thatcher was too weary to protest. He, Wyatt and Natalie stepped quickly out into the cool night. The sooner he moved the truck and got Juniper, the sooner they could all make the hour-long drive home. The day had been exhausting and full—

So full, he had forgotten about Natalie's big news, but at least he remembered it now.

"Congratulations, man. A baby, wow." His smile for Wyatt was real, but in his fatigue, he could tell it didn't reach his eyes. Hopefully Wyatt wouldn't notice in the long shadows cast by the glow of the lampposts.

Wyatt shoved his hands into his jacket pockets. "It wasn't the way we planned to tell you all, but it's okay. Natalie filled me in on what happened today. About Asa, too."

Thatcher braced for a lecture—one he completely deserved. "I'm sorrier than you'll ever know. I never would have said anything if I had known she was pregnant. I hate that I upset her and made her sick."

"I'm right here," Natalie reminded them. "And I told you I was already sick regardless."

"Seriously," Wyatt agreed. "I made her sick yesterday by frying sausage for breakfast."

"But I dropped an emotional bomb."

"I'm okay, Thatcher." Natalie's words formed vapor in the cool evening. "And so is Juniper, and right now, that's the most important thing."

"Are you sure you're okay?"

"Physically, yes, despite this constant nausea. Emotionally? I'll be honest. It's going to take a while. You and I are the same age, Thatcher. I keep thinking of my mom and how hurt she's going to be when she finds out."

"I know. Aunt Yvonne didn't deserve what Asa did to her. Honestly, I would understand if you wanted to see the back of me. And I couldn't blame Bliss if she felt that way, either. I'll never forgive myself for not watching my words when Juniper was in the vicinity. It's because of me that she ran off."

"Parenthood is rough, Thatcher." Natalie shrugged deeper into her coat. "I've made more mistakes in the past two years than I ever did in my whole life up until this point."

"That's because you're a perfectionist and probably only made one mistake your whole life until then." He couldn't help but tease.

"Very funny, but I admit I'm a total control freak. If I could, I would dress the twins in armor so they don't even stub their toes, but I have to trust God to protect them when I can't, because I make mistakes."

Wyatt folded his arms. "Did we ever tell you how I lost track of Luna when she was learning to walk? She toddled off at my parents' ranch."

"No." Thatcher would remember that story if they had told him.

"I was livid," Natalie admitted, "but he wasn't being irresponsible. Luna wasn't walking…until she was, the very moment he looked away for two seconds. I realized—and he did, too—that while we need to be as careful as possible, life isn't perfect. We can do all the right things, and bad things still happen."

Thatcher turned them into a separate section of the visitor lot. "I don't do all the right things, though."

"So you've learned a lesson." Wyatt's tone was deep with emotion. "Cut yourself some slack, man. You're an imperfect human being who has been a parent for all of what, five weeks? Most people experience a slower learning curve. They get nine months to prepare for a baby and then grow along with them. Give yourself time."

"I'm not sure time will help. What if I'm too much like Asa or Jake to be any good at this? Maybe I've only been concerned about myself for so long that I can't change." They were close enough to the truck for him to click the button on the fob and unlock it.

Wyatt's incredulous face was briefly lit up by the orange flash of Thatcher's blinking taillights. "You've changed a lot in two months. Mistakes and bad consequences used to roll off you like April showers off a mallard's back. Now you're punishing yourself."

"Because there's a kid at stake."

"That's exactly Wyatt's point." Natalie smiled as she slipped into the cab's front seat. As soon as Thatcher sat behind the wheel, she turned to him. "My dad was in it for himself, no matter what was at stake or who got hurt. Even if it was a vulnerable kid who loved him and needed him."

"The fact that you're concerned about parenting Juniper shows how unlike Asa you are, man." Wyatt's tone was emphatic from the back seat. "Forgive yourself for whatever part you may have played in her running off, but don't forget you weren't exactly having that conversation in front of her. She overheard."

"I'd said I couldn't be a decent dad. She thought I meant I was going to leave her and Bliss." The words were hard and jagged as rocks in his throat. "But I was thinking that, too."

"Because you and Bliss aren't together that way?"

"Yes." He backed out of the spot.

"But you care about Juniper," Wyatt noted.

"I love her."

"We know you do. It's obvious." A faint smile played about Wyatt's lips. "You love Bliss, too."

"No," Thatcher started.

"We're not saying *how* you love her, but there's something between you two." Natalie waggled her finger. "During the family meeting where you told us about Dad, you clung to her like she was an anchor in the storm. You need her, and I think she needs you, too."

Did she? "She only married me so she could adopt Juniper."

"That doesn't mean I'm wrong."

"They deserve better than me, though. I'm following too much in the Dalton men's footsteps."

"Because you dated a lot? Because you share the same natural ability to run the ranch? Maybe, but I see differences between you and Asa. Big ones." Natalie adjusted the heater as he drove through the parking lot. "One, you're a good son to Doreen, and Asa wasn't on speaking terms with his mother. Two, you've got an entrepreneurial spirit and a vision that exceeds his. You want to expand the ranch, and he limited Foxtail's operations, from the bakery to the ranch, by keeping them all under his control."

"I'm not sure if the latter means I'm greedy or dissatisfied, but the land is going to waste—"

"I'm not finished." Natalie's tone was more insistent than he'd ever heard before. "The situation right now with Juniper? If it was one of us, Asa wouldn't have even been here. I guarantee you that he wouldn't lose a wink of sleep worrying about his kid or wondering what he could've done differently. But you, Thatcher Dalton, own your actions. You accept blame and seek forgiveness when you make a mistake, and then you make amends. Right there, that sets you head and shoulders apart from our father."

Thatcher pulled up in front of the hospital and set his hazard lights, unsure what to say.

But Natalie wasn't finished, anyway.

"More than that, though, you gave your life to God. An active, loving, transformative God who is with you."

Wyatt leaned forward between their seats. "He alone can give you the strength to be the man He wants you to be, brother. And I say that as a former addict who ruined everything I touched for a while there. But look at me now. Because of God, I'm a sober man who's raising children who aren't mine biologically, but they're mine in my heart. And I know you feel that way about Juniper."

"I do. And I pray she knows it by my words and actions, every day."

Wyatt opened the door, allowing cold air to slither into the cab. "I see Mick pulling into the lot."

"And there are my girls." Bliss, holding Coco's leash, walked alongside Dove and a muscular young orderly who pushed Juniper in the wheelchair. Thatcher turned off the ignition and leaped out to meet them. “Hey. Ready to go home?”

Juniper reached up to him with both arms. He lifted her from the wheelchair and carried her to the back seat. Coco hopped up beside her, and Thatcher gave the pup a quick rub over her head and neck. “Good girls, both of you.”

“Here you go.” Sadie ran up, holding out a paper bag. “The selection wasn’t great, but it should tide you over. Plus, we found some sour cream doughnuts for dessert.”

“Thanks.” Thatcher gave her a side hug while Bliss took the bag.

“See you tomorrow?” Natalie’s eyes were tired, but wide with unspoken emotion.

“Yes.” Thatcher hugged her. “Thanks for being here. All of you.”

“We’re family.”

Even though their family looked and felt far different than it had two months ago.

Thatcher wasn’t sure who he was anymore or how he fit into any of his relationships. But he did know God was still active, still present, and that there was something very, very important he had to do.

So, once they were home and Juniper tucked into bed, he reached for Bliss. For an instant, he thought she’d push him away, but then her hands slipped beneath his jacket and wrapped around his back, her hands cold through the fabric of his shirt.

She smelled of the hospital and, faintly, of her fruity shampoo. A smell that meant home to him now. He bent to better inhale it, and he kissed her crown, right where the part divided her straight blond locks. He hoped she drew comfort from him as he drew it from her.

"I'm sorry," he whispered into her hair.

"Me, too." Her voice was muffled against his shirt.

He didn't want to let go, but he had to, now, before he did something foolish like decide to never let her go. So with one last kiss atop her head, he released her. "I'll lock up for the night. You go on to bed. You must be exhausted."

"Thank you. Goodnight, then." It was impossible to read her expression.

Hopefully, she couldn't read his, because he was thinking about what Natalie and Wyatt said. That he loved her.

He couldn't. Not in a way other than the love of a friend.

He had messed up more than enough. No more distractions, and that included his attraction to her. Juniper's happiness was at stake, and he wouldn't allow anything like tonight's scare with Juniper to happen again…not because of his foolishness.

Chapter Eleven

A week later, Bliss was elbow deep in carving a watermelon to look like a flower basket. When her phone buzzed, she accepted the call without pausing to look at the screen.

"Thatcher? Where are you? Juniper's party starts in fifteen minutes." He had promised to help set it up. Thankfully, his family and Olivia were pitching in, but that wasn't the point. He should be here.

Something had obviously come up on the ranch that required extra attention. Or he was hurt. Because surely he hadn't forgotten. Not after Asa forgot *his* birthday party, and he knew firsthand how hurt Juniper would be if he didn't show up.

"Bliss?" The voice wasn't Thatcher's. "It's Sterling Brandenburg."

"Oh, Sterling." Bliss tried to hide her disappointment. After all, Sterling and his wife, Evie, had been her only friends when she was in school. "It's lovely to hear from you."

"Small world, eh? When I saw your photo in Vera's room, I couldn't believe it."

Bliss shaded her eyes from the bright noon sun as she scanned the horizon for any sign of Thatcher. "She said you're starting up a bookkeeping business," Bliss said absentmindedly. “Congratulations. I know you’ll do wonderfully.”

“Thanks. But before I say anything more about that, Vera mentioned you were widowed. I’m so sorry about that.”

“Thank you.” She bit her lip. Lane hadn’t been kind to Sterling or Evie.

“She also said you’re looking for something new, careerwise.”

A nice way to allude to Bliss’s being laid off.

Bliss listened while he described the job. “This would have been perfect, but my circumstances have changed. I’m married and adopting Vera’s granddaughter.”

“I completely understand, and congratulations. Family first. But would you be interested in spending part of your summer here to help me get off the ground? We have a guest house in the backyard for you, and your daughter could hang out with our daughters. Plus, you’d be less than a mile from Vera. And I would compensate you for your time.” He named a number.

“Wow.” Everything about this arrangement sounded fantastic...except for how Thatcher fit into it. She knew he couldn’t leave the ranch.

“Let me know after Easter.”

“Sure, Sterling, and thank you.” She caught Olivia’s gaze as her friend strolled toward her. “I’d love to catch up more, but Juniper’s birthday party is about to start.”

“You have my number now. Call when you can. And happy birthday to Juniper.”

“The watermelon looks great, Bliss.” Olivia smoothed the red-and-white-checked tablecloth atop Bliss’s workspace, which would also serve as the food table for the outdoor event. “I set up the photo station. How can I help now?”

"Could you set out plates?" She gestured at a stack of paper goods, then eyed the watermelon. She had cut it in two and hollowed out the halves, then chopped one's rind so it looked like a basket handle. She'd stuck toothpicks in the ends and pushed it into the other half. "I think I'm going to call this good. The kids will be here soon."

"You did a great job." Olivia tore off the plastic packaging from the plates. "Haybale seating, picnic blankets and horses to ride—I never had a party this fun. Where's Juniper? With Thatcher?"

Pushing back against her desire to fret, Bliss reached into the cooler at her feet for a container of chopped mixed fruit. "She's with Natalie and her girls."

"Was that Thatcher on the phone?" Olivia's subtlety didn't disguise her curiosity. She still didn't trust Thatcher; that much was clear.

And Bliss didn't like it. "No." She dumped the fruit into the rind basket. "I haven't seen him since he left for his morning rounds. Honestly, I'm trying not to worry. Something's keeping him away."

Olivia started unwrapping a package of paper cups. "I'm sure it's nothing bad. You know how Thatcher is."

"I do." She stuck a spoon into the fruit and then reached into the cooler for the veggie tray. "He wouldn't forget."

Olivia bit her lip. "Well, he forgot Juniper's dentist appointment. I know it's not the same, but I've known Thatcher for years. He's easily distracted, flirtatious and gets caught by whatever's right in front of him. Seeing how the ranch is his life—the whole reason he married you—it stands to reason that something came up on his rounds and the party slipped his mind."

"He cares about more than the ranch." Every muscle in Bliss's body tensed. Diving back into the cooler for a gallon of lemonade, she fought to watch her words. For so many years, she had stayed silent when confronted, but since Lane died, she had found her voice. She didn't want to use it for harm, but she had to set the record straight. "Why do you expect the worst of Thatcher? Did you date him back in the day?"

Olivia spluttered. "No, this isn't about that. But I was once with someone exactly like him. I want to spare you the same sort of pain I went through."

Bliss's heart softened, recalling Olivia's difficult past, but this situation wasn't the same at all. "I know you don't understand our marriage arrangement, Liv. But Thatcher is not the same man he once was. He's kind, and funny and caring. He's devoted to Juniper. He is *not* Asa."

"I didn't say he was." Olivia reached for Bliss's arm. "Oh, honey. I've never seen you like this. You're in love with Thatcher, aren't you?"

Bliss almost dropped the lemonade pitcher. "Of course not. You know our marriage is a legal thing between friends."

"That doesn't mean you didn't fall in love."

Bliss swiped a blob of watermelon off her denim shirt so she wouldn't have to look Olivia in the eye. "This isn't about me. It's about Thatcher. Something must be wrong, because he would not ditch Juniper."

"Okay, then. I trust you." Olivia's tone was so serious, so rich in apology, that Bliss finally met her gaze. "And if you trust him?"

"I do."

But Olivia had planted a seed of doubt, and it hadn't taken more than a second to sprout, watered by the words Olivia used about him. Words she had heard from others, like *unreliable* and *flirtatious*.

That last one made her feel like the moments of connection they shared didn't mean anything. Like their marriage didn't mean anything.

Which wasn't true, but the only love in their home was their mutual love for Juniper.

He had proven he cared about Juniper, and she had to move forward in faith—for the long-term, as well as the short. Today had to be a happy day for her foster daughter. "Liv, I don't want Juniper to know I'm worried."

"She won't hear it from me." Olivia mimed zipping her lips. "And I'll pray for Thatcher to be okay."

Words failed Bliss, so she simply hugged Olivia.

A few minutes later, her cell phone pinged, but before she could look at it, Thatcher appeared, riding Maverick toward the stable. After asking Olivia to finish setting up the table, she took off at a jog, and by the time she reached the stable, he had the gelding in the crossties. Thatcher's skin was dewy with sweat, and dirt smeared his jeans and forearms as he removed Maverick's saddle.

She threw her arms around him. "Are you okay?"

"I'm fine, just kicking myself for being so late. A calf fell into a ditch. I couldn't leave him like that—he could have died of dehydration. Not to mention his mama was freaking out. It took me a while to get him out, but everything's okay now. I'm really sorry. I texted you so you wouldn't worry, but you know how cell service is out there."

She pulled back, embarrassed by her emphatic display. "My phone just pinged, so that must be your text. Since the cell service is so unreliable, maybe we need to invest in satellite phones or something." She was only half joking.

"Hey." Wyatt appeared, his eyes curious. "It's about time for the party to start. How about I finish putting Maverick away so you can clean up, Thatcher?"

"That would be great." Thatcher turned to Bliss.

"See you in a few." Bliss brushed some of the dirt their hug had transferred to her and hurried back to the party area. She had missed Juniper's arrival, and the now ten-year-old sat with Natalie's twins inside a pen of rabbits Mick had set up on the grass.

Joy shone on their faces and carried on their cries of delight as Juniper, Luna and Rose patted the bunnies. Nearby, Mick tossed a ball to Coco. Bliss was grateful for his consideration of the pup's need for fun before she worked amid the many distractions of the party.

Bliss tamped down the emotional roller coaster inside her and joined Natalie outside the pen. "Well, look at this lovely sight. Three beautiful girls and some bunnies."

"Dis one's soft," Luna told her, pointing to a black-and-white rabbit.

"I wike dem all." Rose patted one on the back.

"Bliss, can we get one?" Juniper pulled a sturdy gray rabbit onto her lap. "They're so cute."

"I thought you wanted a cat." Bliss reached down and touched a midsized bunny with brown-and-white splotches. His ears felt like velvet to her fretful fingers.

"Well, they're both officially now on my Easter wish list, because it's too late for my birthday list." Juniper buried her face in the gray's soft fur.

"I've never heard of an Easter wish." Natalie smiled at Juniper.

"That's because my mom—my first mom—made them up. I know it's better to pray than to wish for something, but I still do it every year because it reminds me of her." Juniper's eyes brightened. "Zoe's here! And that car right there is Jeremiah's. Come on, Coco."

At once, Coco dropped the ball she and Mick had been

playing with and trotted to the rabbit pen, waiting while Juniper let herself out.

Within a few minutes, most of Juniper's class had arrived, as had Dutch and Beatie with Gidget, who was as big of a hit with the kids as the rabbits. Just as Bliss was sending the kids off on a scavenger hunt in groups of two, Thatcher returned, wearing clean jeans and a T-shirt that showed off his muscles in a way she probably shouldn't be noticing.

He jumped right into the festivities, focusing on the kids and the fun. Bliss couldn't have asked for more for Juniper's sake. But for her own?

She yearned for his gaze to land on her. To share a private joke, word or even a smile. She didn't want all of his attention during the party, of course. This was about Juniper. But she wouldn't have minded a fleeting glance, at least.

You're in love with him.

Oh, no. She couldn't be. Didn't want to be. Especially after entertaining the thought that maybe he had forgotten Juniper's party. She knew better. What was wrong with her?

She felt like she was picking petals off a flower, but instead of the old "He loves me, he loves me not," she was spiraling between *I love him, I can't love him*, and *He would never forget Juniper's party, but I thought he might have forgotten.*

She was a mess internally, but she managed to get through the party, and afterwards, order pizza to thank their friends and family who had helped. Once everyone had departed and Juniper had gone to bed, Bliss was more than ready for some peace to think.

As she made herself a mug of chamomile tea, however, Thatcher lingered in the doorway. "It's a nice night. Do you want to sit out on the porch swing?"

See, he's not avoiding you after all. You've been acting silly all day because you lo—

"Sure." Telling her thoughts to knock it off, she grabbed a blanket from the back of the couch. "I wonder if we'll be able to see stars."

Once they were settled on the swing, surrounded by the chirps of night insects and the cool darkness, he pointed ahead. "There's Venus, nice and low on the horizon."

"It's so bright." She cupped her mug, allowing its warmth to seep into her hands. "Juniper had a great time today, and so did her friends. It looked like you did, too."

"I love seeing Juniper happy." Then he let out a long sigh. "My mom called this morning just before I left on my rounds. We've been playing phone tag, and I felt I had to take it."

Oh. He'd been holding it all in so it wouldn't upset the party. "How did the conversation go?"

"Hard. She never wanted me to know the truth, but Asa is my dad. He barely knew my biological mom. When she found out she was pregnant, she told him, and then learned he was married. At that point, she decided to give me up for adoption. That's when Asa suggested she give me to his brother and sister-in-law."

She set her mug down on the ground and took his hands. "That must have been difficult to hear."

"It was a relief, too. But to be honest, that's not the thing weighing on me the most right now." He stretched out his legs and set the swing in motion. "I'm sorry I worried you by showing up late to the party. Did you think I forgot?"

She couldn't lie. "Mainly I was concerned you'd been bitten by a snake or something, but at one point it entered my mind that you could have been distracted. I rejected the thought, but I'm sorry if that hurts you."

"It doesn't feel great, but I don't blame you. I told you that I start off with good intentions, just like Asa did, but I end up blowing everything apart."

"You didn't blow anything apart. You saved a calf and then rushed back for Juniper." Her grip tightened on his arm. "I trust you, Thatcher."

Thatcher's eyes were sad. "Thank you, but I should have found someone else to take care of the calf. I just didn't think it would take as long as it did. That's the thing. I didn't think. Maybe you *shouldn't* trust me."

"Thatcher, you and I have to learn how to live with the realities of life, whether it's calves in ditches or family drama, without you fearing I'll think the worst of you, or me fearing the same of you. Neither of us are perfect. I worry too much and, well, I have my issues. But we're humans, not robots."

"You always make me feel better, Bliss."

"You do the same for me."

"I guess it's good we got married then, isn't it?"

Bliss willed her heart to stop pattering so hard in her chest. They were friends…friends who were helping each other. "It is good. The adoption is progressing, thanks to you. But I'm afraid you're not getting anything you wanted out of this marriage."

"That's not true. I got to keep Foxtail Ranch."

"But you can't do what you want with it. If you'd married someone else, Everest would have granted you the loan."

"But then I wouldn't have Juniper." His nostrils flared, as if the thought of losing his soon-to-be stepdaughter was unbearable. "Or you."

He looked at her then. Really looked at her. Leaned forward so he was a hair's breadth from her. His breath warmed her cheek, flooding her system with adrenaline.

"Bliss?"

"Yes." She answered the question, whatever it was. Hopefully, about kissing her.

"Something has changed between us, hasn't it?" His warm hand cupped her cheek.

How could she deny it when her heart raced so hard and fast that it might pound right out of her chest? "We care about each other."

"Care?" His thumb traced her lower lip.

Olivia was right. This was more than caring. This was something else.

Her hands rested on his chest. No real effort was required to pull him closer and close the gap between their lips.

The kiss was gentle, but she had never felt so cherished, so protected. It was as sweet and precious as she could ever have imagined, and it sealed her feelings for him.

When they parted, she buried her head in his neck, where his pulse thrummed against her ear.

She had fought against herself for a long time, but she conceded defeat.

"I love you," she whispered.

His Adam's apple worked against her forehead, but he said nothing.

He must be as scared as she was. "I love you, and I think you might—"

"No. I can't." He edged back. "As much as I wanted to kiss you, this can't happen again. It will ruin the life we're trying to build for Juniper."

The fire within her sputtered.

Once, she would have felt ashamed of herself for kissing him, but maybe it was for the best that she'd done it. Otherwise, she would still be lying to herself about her feelings, and now she knew where they stood.

She also had the Lord to help her heal from the pain of unrequited love, and a voice to speak for herself.

So, she started folding the blanket, slowly, neatly.

"Do you remember Vera telling me about a job in San Diego? Well, I heard from my old friend Sterling today. He offered me the position. I told him no, but then he invited me and Juniper to come for the summer so I can help him get his business off the ground. I think I should accept."

Thatcher recoiled as if she had struck him. "You would take Juniper, after all the upheaval she's had? This is her home now."

"It will only be for a few weeks, and then we'll come back. We're a family, Thatcher, but it might not hurt to have some time apart so we can think about how we'll move forward in the future. And so I can…reset my emotions." Maybe the lack of his daily presence around her would help her love dry up like a raisin on the vine.

"I promised I'd always be there for you. I can't do that if we don't live in the same town."

"It's only an hour's drive. That's nothing. But I promise you, Thatcher, you and I will always be there for each other. We just can't go on the way we have been. I don't want to ruin anything." She used his words, hoping he would understand.

"You could never do that, Bliss."

"I almost did just now." She rose, gathering the blanket and her cold, untouched tea from the ground. "It'll be okay, Thatcher. I promise."

Even though it didn't feel like it at all.

The following week felt like the longest of Thatcher's life.

Days at the ranch house were cordial, full of polite *please*s and *thank-you*s when he and Bliss interacted. The calendar page turned to April and, with Juniper off school for spring break, Thatcher spent as much time with her as possible. They baked Resurrection Cookies, sweet, hollow meringues that echoed the empty Easter tomb. They also decorated the living room for the holiday. Now, the hearth boasted an Easter banner, taper candles that looked like carrots and a porcelain cross that said *He is Risen.*

The festive additions touched a place inside him he hadn't known existed. This little house had truly become a home.

But was he losing Bliss and Juniper? Bliss promised they'd come back after their summer jaunt, but Thatcher felt like there was a permanent wedge between them since he'd told her he couldn't love her. It was to protect her from inevitably being hurt by him, but it had hurt her, nonetheless.

He had warned her that he was too much like Asa, and sure enough, he'd gone and hurt her. He had forgotten himself and willingly, eagerly kissed her back.

He wouldn't deny he was drawn to Bliss. More than he'd ever been drawn to any woman. But he cared more about her happiness than his own, and wanted to treat her with the greatest respect and kindness.

Maybe the Lord was changing him for the better, after all. At least that was a comforting thought.

The day before Easter, sleep eluded him, so he rose before dawn, gulped down a cup of strong coffee and tiptoed out of the house as fingers of purple and gold touched the eastern horizon.

He fed the horses, then saddled Maverick and rode out as the sky lightened over the spring-green world. The north fence line probably didn't need checking, but he went there, anyway.

He dismounted to get a closer look. Sure enough, the

fence looked fine, with no new breaks. He stared over the fence at the acres of Foxtail land he had long dreamed of possessing. Yet rather than dwell on the plans he had for it, he was overcome with memories of bringing Bliss here.

Thatcher shook his head at himself. He may not have been able to expand the boundary, or plant alfalfa or any of the other things that would help him turn a decent profit, but he had gained far more than he'd lost due to Asa's demand that he marry.

A daughter in Juniper. A best friend in Bliss.

Oh, Bliss. He wished he didn't think of her every second. Or that when they were in the house, he wasn't aware of her every movement. He had thought he could escape thoughts of her out here, in a place that used to be a refuge from his troubles, but that was a foolish idea.

Lord, I don't know how You can repair the gap between us, but I trust You. You've changed me so I'm no longer the man I once was. Help me grow more and more in Christ's likeness, and be the man You want me to be.

Maverick's sharp snort drew him around. The gelding pawed the ground, his alert ears curved ahead of him like satellite dishes. Thatcher scanned the horizon for the source of his horse's distress, but saw nothing. He patted the bay's thick neck. "What's got you spooked, Mav?"

He couldn't see anything moving in the grass, but there could be a snake. A little early in the day for one, true, but—

It wasn't too early for whatever moved just now in the oak tree.

There it was again, flicking below a branch. A thick, buff, black-tipped tail.

His gaze searched higher. It was half camouflaged by leaves, but there was no mistaking the sleek, tawny coat of a mountain lion. Sprawled atop one of the branches, it lounged in the perfect position for hunting prey or resting before returning to its den for the day.

Either way, Thatcher would give it wide berth.

He had never heard of a mountain lion attacking a horse. Undoubtedly, it happened on occasion, but the lion could find prey easier elsewhere. Maverick clearly wanted to get away, but Thatcher had a different idea. He opened his saddlebag and pulled out a can of bear spray, should the need arise.

As he did so, Maverick shifted, clearly uneasy. “Easy does it, Mav. He’s not interested in us.”

As he spoke, however, the mountain lion dropped from the tree with a soft thud. It didn’t approach but stared at him with unblinking green eyes. It was curious…or daring Thatcher to make the first move.

The standoff gave Thatcher the opportunity to study it. The male was young, which probably accounted for Thatcher mistaking the paw prints for those of a female. It didn’t appear hungry or ill, thankfully.

“Go on, now,” Thatcher ordered the cat, his tone stern. Then, with the hand holding the can of bear spray, he opened his coat and held it out to make himself look bigger. “It’s time to move on.”

The mountain lion’s ears swiveled south. So did Maverick’s. Thatcher shifted his gaze in that direction, too, without moving his body.

Please, not another mountain lion, Lord.

Instead, beneath another oak thirty or forty feet away, a gray fox watched them. Not a single hair on it seemed to twitch.

“Go on, buddy.” Thatcher didn’t want the little critter—the namesake of Foxtail Farm and Ranch—getting hurt. Why didn’t the fox scamper off? Maybe something was wrong with it, but like the mountain lion, it showed no obvious sign of injury or disease.

The mountain lion's ears curved back toward Thatcher. Then, as if it decided neither he nor the fox were worth its time, it turned and loped off, jumping over the fence in one smooth, powerful leap.

Thatcher let out a sigh of relief and repacked the bear spray. When he looked back up, the fox was gone, too.

Shaking his head at the oddness of it all, he patted Maverick's neck in long, soothing strokes. "I know that was spooky, Mav, but this is that cat's land as much as it is ours. We have to share it peacefully. But I think I'll be picking up the pace to get those livestock guard dogs. And extend the height on our permanent fence."

If he could afford to do that, without the loan.

As Thatcher watched the big cat grow smaller and smaller as it loped off, he felt as if they had come to an understanding of sorts. Neither of them meant harm to the other, and both wanted to protect and provide for their own.

While Thatcher never intended to let his guard down, he knew that he and the mountain lion could coexist.

Maybe, in a similar way, he could coexist with the long shadow Asa cast over him. He could acknowledge the tendencies he had inherited from both Asa and Jake, while at the same time choosing to keep his guard up against those tendencies. He could trust God to guide him. and maybe it was time to truly forgive Jake and Asa.

It wouldn't be easy, but maybe he wouldn't be free of the past until he sought God's help to do so.

Right there in the pasture, surrounded by gentle moos and Maverick's soft breaths, he dropped to his knees.

Lord, I'm sorry for holding grudges against Asa and Jake. Pastor Luke says forgiveness is sometimes a daily choice, but I never wanted to think about it too much. Probably because I didn't want to forgive them. And because I hate the ways I've acted just like them. But you are a God of transformation, and You are working in me. I see that now, and I'm grateful.

He prayed so long he lost track of the minutes, but it was the best he had felt in ages. After asking forgiveness for himself and the grace to forgive others, he felt cleaner, more hopeful and blessed.

And he also realized something deep in his bones. As much as he loved Foxtail, as much as it was woven into his being—it wasn't worth anything without Bliss and Juniper.

The expansion didn't matter. Thatcher could continue scraping by for the next two years in compliance with Asa's original will so that Natalie, Sadie and Dove could inherit their portions of the farm operation.

Once all four of their inheritances were guaranteed, he should forget about expanding Foxtail Ranch and just walk away. Sell his stock and start over somewhere new. As much as he loved Foxtail, he couldn't improve it without a loan. He could move forward as his own man, on his own terms, with the most important thing in his life.

His new family.

He recommitted to being there for Juniper. He would not allow history to repeat itself just because Asa's blood pounded through his veins.

And he wanted to recommit to Bliss, too.

But what would he do if Bliss got to San Diego and she and Juniper decided they were happier there? What if she decided to make that job permanent?

Juniper wasn't his adopted daughter. He had no rights to her, although Bliss had been emphatic that he remain in Juniper's life.

Regardless, God hadn't brought him this far only to abandon him. Resolving to pray and trust, hoisted himself back into the saddle. "Let's go home, Mav."

Maverick seemed only too happy to oblige. The gelding trotted at a steady pace, and it wasn't long before they were back in the barn.

Some of the hands were already there, but Thatcher saw to Maverick's tack himself. After giving him a thorough brushing, Thatcher set him out in the paddock with the other horses. Then he pulled out his phone and scrolled through his contacts until he found Pastor Luke's phone number. Holy Week was among the busiest times of a pastor's schedule, he knew, but this couldn't wait.

He shot him a text and returned to the ranch house. Bliss and Juniper would be awake by now. He didn't know what he would say or how to move forward, but he was confident they would both appreciate a pancake breakfast.

He removed his crusty boots on the porch and snuck inside. It was so quiet he thought they might have decided to sleep in after all, until he saw their cereal bowls in the dish drainer and the note propped up on the table.

"On errands" was all it said.

And he couldn't help wondering if he had come to the realization about how much he wanted them to be his family far too late.

Chapter Twelve

"Are you okay, Bliss?"

At Olivia's question, Bliss tore her gaze away from Juniper, who examined the latch-hook kits for sale in Olivia's store. Coco, ever faithful, stood in her blue service-dog vest at Juniper's side, relaxed but focused. Bliss turned back to Olivia and forced a smile. "I'm fine. Are you sure you don't mind if Juniper and Coco hang out with you for a few minutes? I only planned to drop in so she could pick out a new kit."

"I wouldn't have offered if I didn't love spending time with Juniper. Besides, the store is quiet, and she and I haven't hung out in a while. You can call me any time to check on us, if you're worried about her."

Bliss appreciated her friend's support. "It's not that. I hope you know that if I'm ever concerned about her, it's not that I don't trust you. It's life I don't trust."

"As long as you're still trusting God, that's the most important thing." Olivia patted Bliss's shoulder. "He's the only One who never lets us down."

"I know." Bliss glanced back at Juniper. "But sometimes, I don't trust Him as well as I wish I did. I want to hold her close and not let go."

"But then she couldn't grow. And neither could you."

"Do you ever wish you could *not* grow? Do you wish you could stay shallow, unfazed by any troubles at all?" Bliss chuckled at the absurdity of her statement. "I know that's not how we grow, though. And I'm glad God didn't leave me where I was when I first met Him. I was lost and afraid to make any waves."

"I remember how timid you were when you moved to town. Determined to be independent, but the slightest harsh word would set you back. Look at you now, though, giving me what for about Thatcher."

"What do you mean?"

"You defended him to me at Juniper's party."

True. The old Bliss wouldn't have done that. "I've certainly made waves lately. I told Thatcher some things that weren't easy to say."

"Like what?" Olivia's eyes grew wide.

Oh, no. She did not want to tell her friend that she'd dropped the L-word on Thatcher.

"Bliss?" Juniper joined them, holding a rabbit latch-hook kit. "I pick this one."

"Excellent choice." Bliss enveloped Juniper in a big hug. "Have fun making it with Olivia. I love you."

"Love you, too."

Bliss bent to Coco and rubbed her cheeks with both hands. "I love you too, Coco. Take care of our girl." Words she often said, but she realized she should never leave it there. She should be thanking God for Coco in these times and asking for God's protection and care for both Juniper *and* her dog. God, after all, was the One who truly held them all in His hand.

But as she left them at Olivia's craft store to shop for tomorrow's Easter meal, she couldn't help but replay her conversation with Olivia about how she had defended Thatcher.

She would eagerly defend him and Juniper to anyone, any time. But she had never been able to defend herself in the past. She had reminded Thatcher that he was a beloved child of God. Well, she was, too, wasn't she?

And she shouldn't be afraid of making that clear to Everest. It was time she helped Thatcher achieve his goals by having a candid conversation with her former father-in-law.

Her other errands could wait. She marched east on Sycamore, then turned the corner. A short block later, she strode up the concrete walkway to Goldenrod's bank, a sturdy yellow brick building with white pilasters and ornamentation that made Bliss think of a grand English manor—which was probably the point. It instilled confidence and stability over the passage of time.

In her marriage to Lane, however, she had learned that facades and veneers, whether fixed on buildings or put on by people, should never be trusted to reflect what lay beneath them.

It had taken her a while to appreciate that Thatcher had no facade at all. There was no pretense in him, and he couldn't mask his emotions or disguise his thoughts with flattery if he tried.

He grieved his mistakes, but to Bliss, the fact that he acknowledged them and strove not to repeat them was more precious than gold. His honesty was a gift, even when it hurt. Like when he told her he couldn't love her.

But she loved him, and she could give him this gift.

The main room had been painted the color of bay leaves. The two desks on one end of the room were empty, but a single teller stood behind the dark wooden counter, smiling warmly.

"Good morning. How may I help you?"

Praying for strength, she strode up to the young man

with slicked-back hair. "I'd like to see Everest Sloane, please."

The fellow winced. "I'm sorry, but seeing as it's Saturday, the staff is limited."

"I know he's here. Everest always works on Saturdays." She hoped he still did, anyway. "He's my father-in-law."

"My apologies. I didn't realize you're family." The young man bustled around the counter, smoothing his navy tie as he walked. "This way, please."

She followed him, although she knew right where Everest's office was. They turned down a hallway and the teller rapped on a polished wooden door. When bidden, he thrust it open. "Pardon the interruption, but your daughter-in-law is here."

The poor fellow must be new here, because he smiled widely, as if he expected Everest to be happy with this development. The disapproving rumble emanating from Everest's fleshy throat caused the young man to flush.

Bliss didn't want him to get into trouble, so she strode straight past him into the room. "This will only take a minute, Everest."

Everest waved the teller away with a brusque shoo of his knobby fingers.

"Hello, Bliss." His heavy eyelids closed halfway as he peered at her. "Or should I call you Mrs. Dalton?"

Once, she would have lowered her gaze, deferred to him in tone and manner. But that was over now.

"I thought you must have heard about my marriage, since you denied my husband a loan."

"Did I? I'm a busy man, Bliss. Too busy to look over every single application we receive, and we receive plenty. I don't concern myself with you and I haven't in years. You're dismissed."

Her resolve wobbled, but she squared her shoulders so she would look braver than she felt. "I know you look at everything that passes through this bank, and I can't help but believe your reasons for turning down Thatcher were personal, rather than professional."

His jowls quivered. "I'm not sure how you could prove such a thing."

"I'm not interested in proving anything. I'm only here to ask you to reconsider."

"Your husband sent you, eh? Not quite the strong man he looks like, is he?"

"He doesn't know I'm here."

"Well, I'm not changing my mind. What are you going to do about it?" He looked rather pleased with himself, as if he hoped she would cower and beg.

"Nothing."

Disappointment flickered in his eyes. "Then why did you bother barging your way in here?"

"I already told you. To ask you to reconsider, because you are the only bank in town. We both know there are other banks, but your proximity would make Thatcher's life a lot easier." She shrugged. "He's a good man and dependable for that loan. But if you refuse, as I said, there are other banks. And if they turn us down, I trust God to provide if, and when, He chooses."

"You say he's dependable, but the ranch is struggling, and all you have to your name is a dead pear orchard you should have sold ages ago. Oh, yes, I know exactly how much money sits in your savings account. And how much your *husband* has." The way Everest said Thatcher's title was like a hiss.

"We are defined by more than what we own, Everest."

"That's obvious, because his ranch is never going to

amount to anything, no matter how much he borrows to make improvements. Same with the entire farm enterprise. Asa Dalton should've sold it or just picked one of those kids to run things when he died, not four. That farm and ranch are a disaster, all too bound up in the family."

"Bound up in family," she repeated.

"That's what I said." Everest spat out the words. "You always were a bit slow, Bliss."

"It certainly took me long enough to see Lane for who he was." She gathered her purse from the chair beside her. "And some time to find my voice."

He sputtered as if he couldn't think of a word to say.

She had one more thing to tell him on her way out, though. "Thank you. What you said about Foxtail being 'bound up' in family? You've been immensely helpful, Everest. Have a good day."

She hastened into the hallway and out to the main room, where she waved at the abashed teller on her way out. "Happy Easter."

Once she returned to her car, she felt as if she had set down a weight she had been carrying for ten years.

Thank You, Lord.

She prayed in the car—for Juniper, Thatcher, Coco and the Daltons. For Olivia and other friends. For Everest and her parents. She should try reaching out to them again. And she must keep praying for them.

But right now, instead of driving to the grocery store, or even Olivia's, she drove straight toward home.

Good thing Bluetooth was activated in her car, because she had some phone calls to make.

A few hours later, Thatcher pulled his truck into the long driveway of Bliss's grandpa's house. Minutes ago, when he received Bliss's text asking if he could come over, he hadn't known what to expect.

But it sure wasn't Bliss and a host of familiar faces working on the fence between the orchard and Foxtail Ranch.

As he got out of the truck, Bliss practically skipped toward his truck, hammer still in hand. "Surprise."

She sounded excited, but wary, as if unsure if he would approve. But why wouldn't he approve of her fixing her grandpa's half rotten fence—

Wait, she wasn't fixing it. A large section of it was all but gone. "What's all this?"

"A little renovation." She gestured with the hammer at the people behind her. Olivia, Dutch and members of his family. Some held tools. Others continued to tug apart loosened fence rails with their hands. All of them looked in Thatcher's direction, however, as if they were eager to see his reaction. "Your whole family is here, except for Natalie. She's with Rose, Luna, Juniper and Coco, dyeing Easter eggs. Keeping little hands—and Coco's paws—safe from stray nails and splinters."

He still didn't understand. "I would've done any renovations you wanted, Bliss."

"Not when we're trying to surprise you. Don't you see? We're tearing down the fence between my property and yours so you can expand the ranch in this direction. I know it's not the same as expanding over the north boundary, where the grass is literally greener, as you like to say, but it's a start, until you get a loan."

For the first time in his life, Thatcher was literally speechless.

Her smile fell. "You hate this, don't you?"

"No, I definitely do not hate it." He reached for her then, wrapping an arm around her shoulder as they faced their watching family and friends. "If I'm not smiling, it's because I'm absolutely astonished by this. By you."

"Are you sure? Because if you're worried about choking hazards for the cattle, you should know there hasn't been any fruit on these old trees in a long time. My grandpa never used pesticides, so chemicals aren't a concern. Frank popped by and assured me the land was suitable for grazing."

"Frank is in on this?" His voice was so thick with emotion, it was almost hoarse.

"I called a lot of people this morning. After I confronted Everest."

"You talked to Sloane?" His mood shifted from humbled to dangerous in a blink. "Bliss, you shouldn't have had to go through that alone. How awful was he?"

"He tried to grumble at me, but if he thinks he can exert any control over me, the way Lane did, then it's too bad for him. I'm free of that now."

"Free like a butterfly." And just as pretty. "I'm proud of you. But you didn't have to prove yourself to him, or to me, by talking to him."

"I'd rather talk about the fence coming down. I'm sorry I didn't think of it earlier, but Everest said two things that stuck with me, believe it or not. One was that everything in Foxtail is bound up in family—a family I'm now a part of. And the second was a reminder that I own this orchard, and I can do whatever I want with it. And I want to share it with you."

"What if you want to grow pears again?"

"Then I'll plant a few trees by the house." She gestured at the still fenced yard and garden. "You know I want to live here again."

"I was planning on doing that with you, you know."

"Things have changed since then, and I don't want to assume—"

"I'm going with you, Bliss. Not just to this house. To San Diego, if you decide to make things permanent with Sterling."

Bliss's jaw literally dropped. "What are you talking about?"

"It sounds like a good job with good people. Plus, it's close to Vera *and* Juniper's epileptologist. If you want it, you should take it. I have to work the ranch until Asa's will is satisfied, but until I'm free to sell it and join you permanently, I can be with you on weekends."

She stared back at him, confusion in her eyes, but hopefully she was catching on. Could she read in his eyes what he was really saying? How much he—

"Ow!"

He blinked, then looked down. She had dropped the hammer on herself.

"Bliss! Are you okay?"

"I guess I'm not wearing my heels to church tomorrow," she joked, but he wasn't fooled. There was probably a bruise blooming beneath her tennis shoe.

"You need ice."

He twisted around, hooked one arm beneath her knees and the other behind her back, and up she went, into his arms, as if she weighed no more than one of the fence rails.

"What are you doing?" Her tone sounded aghast, but he couldn't help but notice that she snuggled into him.

"I think it's obvious. I'm carrying you inside."

"Want some help in there? I'm a vet if you need me to bandage anything," Mick yelled after them in a teasing tone, followed by Sadie's sharp *shh*.

"Ugh." Bliss moaned. "This is so embarrassing."

"Why? The hammer on your foot?"

"No, the way everyone assumes this is something more than…you know."

"I don't know." He couldn't help but tease.

"You're helping me so I don't have to hop into the house on one foot like a wounded bird."

Thatcher shifted so he could push open the door to her grandpa's house, and then he carried her straight to the living room couch and set her down gently. Then he scooted the soft cream-colored ottoman over for her to prop her foot on.

"Thanks, just need a second to take off my shoe." She bent forward.

"I'll do it."

With the same care he'd shown when setting her down, he knelt in front of the couch and took her ankle in his hands. After loosening the laces, he slipped the shoe from her foot.

"This is like a reverse Cinderella," she joked. "But I'm no princess."

And this was no fairy tale. But that didn't mean it couldn't end happily.

He shouldn't get carried away, though. Bliss was in pain. He left her to go into the kitchen for some ice. "We can go to the ER."

"But I don't exactly care about my foot right now," she hollered after him. "You're *not* moving to San Diego."

He returned with the ice pack and a black-and-white houndstooth dish towel. "We're a family now. You, me and Juniper. The ranch isn't nearly as important as my family is."

"As much as I appreciate your commitment to Juniper, it's a moot point, since I'm only planning on helping Sterling for a few weeks this summer. After that, well, I have news. An hour ago, Pastor Luke offered me a part-time job as the new church office manager." All trace of pain left her face as she grinned.

"That's amazing, but—no buts, I'm just so proud of you and happy for you, Bliss. If it's what you want. I always—only—want your happiness." He wrapped the ice pack in the towel and placed it, oh so gently, atop her foot. "And I'm shocked, because I was just with Pastor Luke, helping him set up the Easter cross for tomorrow's service. He didn't say anything."

"I told him I wanted to tell you myself."

It was a blessing, but not if it didn't fit her plans. "Do you want that job?"

"I do. It's the perfect fit with Juniper's schedule, and I'll still have plenty of time to keep Foxtail's books, so don't worry about that." Her smile faded and she met his gaze. "Juniper has such a beautiful family here. Aunts, uncles, cousins. And a father. Why would I ever want to tear her away from them? From you? And why would I ever tear you from Foxtail Ranch? This is your home, Thatcher. So. I'm not going to hold you to our deal any longer."

"Our deal?" His heart started to pound and he sat beside her. "Are you talking about our marriage vows? Because we said we wouldn't divorce—"

"No, but things have changed."

"You're right. I broke my promise by kissing you."

"Kissing me *back*, maybe, but I'm the one who instigated it. And I will never do it again. I just wanted you to know that I heard you, and I can live with putting the kiss in the past. But if my…my feelings make you uncomfortable, and living together is too awkward for you? That's the deal I'm talking about. I can move back into my grandpa's house, and you can stay at the ranch."

"No way."

"No?"

"No way did you instigate the kiss." He stared into her eyes. "I did."

"I literally grabbed your shirt and pulled."

"I leaned so far over that I was practically almost kissing you before that."

"Almost isn't the same. I'm the one who started it."

"Bliss, I wanted to kiss you. I've wanted to kiss you forever, and I want to kiss you again. Right now." He shifted on the couch and reached for her hands. "But if I do, I can't stop at one. I've been lying to myself for a while now, out of plain, dumb fear. I'm not scared of much in this world, but falling in love for the first time in my life has about done me in."

"You *love* me?"

"I do. And I never knew it was possible to love another person this much. Admitting it to myself was scary." His grip on her hands tightened. "But not half as frightening as the thought of living without you. I'm so sorry I hurt you. Is there a chance you could still love me, after all I put you through?"

"Oh, Thatcher. I don't think I could stop loving you if I tried."

"I want a life with you, Bliss. A real marriage, founded on Jesus, and to that end, I want to go through the marriage counseling with you and Pastor Luke."

"I do, too. But there's sort of an elephant in the room."

"Are you worried about Juniper? Or that I'm not trustworthy?" Like Asa and Jake?

"Those are not concerns at all. I trust you with everything. My daughter, my heart, all of it. No, it's me. If you love me, if you want a real life together?"

"I do." He kissed her hands, one after the other.

"You know I probably can't have children. The doctor said it's not impossible, but with my track record, I have to make sure you understand."

"Oh, honey." Thatcher scooched closer and pulled her into his arms, tucking her head beneath his chin. "Does sitting like this hurt your foot?"

"I pretty much forgot about my foot when you said you loved me."

"Good." He smiled, breathing in her shampoo. "As for kids, we have a kind, smart, beautiful daughter already. And we can have more kids through foster care and adoption. There's no limit to what God can do in our family."

"You're sure?"

"Life doesn't work on a plan. I've learned that firsthand. We have to trust God, hold on and walk in faith."

"For better or for worse." She snuggled against his chest. "We already made those vows, but they take on new meaning today."

"We may have started out as two friends with a plan of what the future would look like, but I'm so glad Asa made up that ridiculous will, because it got me here, to you. I love you, and I trust God to make our family what He wants it to be. If it ends up being the three of us, plus Coco and that cat Juniper wants, well, how blessed are we?"

"And a rabbit, maybe."

"Anything she wants." He chuckled. "You and Juniper are more than I ever dreamed of. You, Bliss, are my precious, kind, smart, beautiful wife, and I want the whole world to know how much I love you."

He paused, committing this moment, the joy of her in his arms, to his memory. Not just in his brain, but his heart.

"I love you, too." She sounded happy. "Now, are you going to kiss me?"

He shifted and drew her face toward his. A moment before his lips touched hers, he smiled. "You will never, ever need to ask me twice."

When he pulled back sometime later, he saw a lifetime of joy and love in her blue eyes.

"I'll hold you to that, husband of mine."

"But for now?" His lips turned into the smile she so dearly loved. "Are you thinking what I'm thinking?"

"Juniper?"

He stood and scooped her into his arms, sending the ice pack to the floor with a thump.

"I *can* probably walk," she said.

"I know. I just like carrying you." He kissed her forehead. "Let's go pick up our girl. I want the rest of our lives as a family to start right now."

Neither of them expected any of this when they got married, but with her in his arms, he could only thank God for the blessings He had bestowed on them. And with Juniper's adoption looming, he knew there would be more blessings from His hand.

Of all the many things to praise God for on Easter tomorrow—the resurrection of His Son, His victory over sin and death, and the promise of eternal life—Bliss added her family to her list. Because this was going to be an Easter she would never forget.

Epilogue

Easter Sunday, One Year Later

With baskets in hand, a few dozen children scampered over the lush green lawn in front of the church, screeching with delight. Juniper ran past with her little cousins, Rose and Luna, hunting for treat-filled plastic eggs hidden behind trees and beneath azalea bushes.

And of course, Coco was right with them, a doggy smile on her sweet face. Juniper hadn't had a seizure in four months, but Coco remained ever vigilant, a blessing and source of comfort.

"Look at them go." Thatcher wrapped an arm around Bliss's shoulders. "What a good day this is. A powerful message at church, some of my favorite hymns and now we get to watch this. I understand why you didn't want to miss Easter Sunday, but it might not hurt you to sit down, babe. It's only been a few weeks since you were in the hospital."

"It wasn't like I had surgery. I just had a baby. I'm fine." She stood on tiptoe to peer into the tiny, blanket-wrapped bundle snuggled tenderly in Thatcher's strong arms. "And he is, too, safe with his daddy."

After so many disappointments in her marriage to Lane, Bliss hadn't believed she was pregnant at first. In fact, she was so certain that she was dealing with another cyst that she was shocked when the doctor told her.

Thatcher supported her the whole pregnancy, especially the long nights when she recalled her two miscarriages and worrying got the best of her. But, as he always did, Thatcher reminded her that he and God were with her, no matter what.

And they were certainly both with her when she delivered Samuel three weeks ago. He was a beautiful baby, if she said so herself, with bright eyes and dark fuzz atop his head that indicated he had inherited his father's hair.

God had grown their family in wonderful ways. Bliss's pregnancy hadn't changed their desire to foster and adopt. They had gone through the necessary preparations and paperwork, and as soon as Samuel was a little older, they would take in a child.

Samuel's older cousin, Natalie's six-month-old baby Elias, watched the older children from the safety of his mother's arms, a slobbery, toothless smile on his sweet face. Sadie, who had been married to Mick for two months now, offered to take him, and Natalie obliged.

"Getting ideas, Sadie?" Thatcher teased her.

"It's in God's hands," she responded. "But yes. Who wouldn't? I can't wait to be a mom."

Dove looked away, but not before Bliss gave her arm a loving squeeze. She hadn't been her cheery self since her long-term boyfriend, Gatlin, abruptly broke up with her a few months ago. All Bliss could do was pray, listen and encourage her as best she could, and she thanked God that Dove had come to church today with the entire family.

As she stood with Thatcher and his sisters, Bliss couldn't help but sneak a peek at the rest of their friends and family, chatting on the patio. Olivia, Doreen, Dutch and Beatie watched the kids from a distance, while Wyatt and Mick both filmed the kids running around. Frank and some of the hands from Foxtail Ranch gathered around the outdoor refreshment table. They were all busier than ever, now that Thatcher had been able to add to the herd, which were well-protected by two new livestock guard dogs named Beau and Charlie.

Bliss couldn't help but wish Vera was here today, but the drive was too hard on her, and her memory continued to slip. Their regular visits and phone calls kept them in close contact, however. Bliss wished her parents had come today, too, but they'd maintained the same disapproving distance they'd started when Lane left her. Nevertheless, Bliss and Thatcher prayed daily for healing.

Yvonne came for Easter, however. Her attendance hadn't been a sure thing, because it had taken a while for her to come to terms with Thatcher being Asa's son. No one could blame her, but her presence was an answer to prayer. Despite all Asa had done to hurt his family, they were all together today, stronger than ever.

Thatcher's mind must be on Asa, too, because he turned to his sisters.

"I finally figured it out."

"Figured what out?" Natalie reached across Sadie to swipe Elias's chin with a soft blue burp cloth.

"Why Asa did what he did, amending his will for me."

"I thought we already knew." Dove's eyebrows knit. "Dad came up with the demand that you marry so you'd settle down."

"To try to change me, yeah. But maybe it was also because he saw potential in me. He didn't want me to settle down, only to be in a failed marriage. He wanted me to be in a successful one. A life he didn't have, and one he knew I wouldn't find if left to my own devices."

Bliss nodded. Asa may not have been a reliable father, but he cared about his children in his own way. "He wanted all of you to be happy, I'm sure of it."

"I think so, now, too. And he knew there would be pain when we found out who I really am. I think he wanted to tie me to the land. To tie me to you, my sisters, so that no matter what happened after we fulfilled the terms of his will, whether we all stay at Foxtail Farm or go our separate ways, we'll be bound together as a family."

"You really think he expected you to find out, after he did such a good job of keeping it a secret for more than thirty years?" Dove bit her lip.

"If he wanted it kept a secret forever, he should have done something with all those boxes full of things Doreen sent him, rather than leave them in plain sight where we could find them." Thatcher shrugged. "I don't think he forgot about them. I think he wanted them found."

"Regardless of why he did it, you're our brother, Thatcher." Natalie came alongside him, smiling first at him, then at little Samuel. "And we love you."

Bliss's eyes filled with tears that had nothing to do with the fatigue of caring for a newborn. "I love this family."

"Mom! Dad! Look at my basket!" Juniper rushed toward Bliss and Thatcher, Coco at her heels, as Rose and Luna rushed to Wyatt.

"Wow, you found a lot of eggs," Bliss marveled.

"Next year I'll help Sammy fill his basket," Juniper added. "Because he'll be walking, right?"

"Right." Thatcher reached out to cup Juniper's shoulder. "He'll be following you everywhere you go because you're his fun big sister."

"He's my Easter wish come true," Juniper said as she peeked inside the blanket holding her baby brother. "I know wishes are just fun, but God really hears our prayers, doesn't He?"

"He does." Bliss met Thatcher's gaze and knew he was as grateful as she for all God had done for them.

Not that long ago, Bliss had had no one in her life. Then God had given her Juniper, then Coco, and then led her to the Dalton family.

Especially Thatcher, whose gaze was soft and tender. "I love you, Bliss."

"I love you, too, Thatcher Dalton. For now and always." She kissed their baby's downy head and leaned into Thatcher's shoulder, watching as Juniper and her precious pup skipped off to romp on the Easter-bright grass.

* * * * *

Dear Reader,

Thank you for joining me at Foxtail Farm once again! I hope you enjoyed spending time with Bliss and Thatcher. He has been a fun secondary character to write in the previous *Home to Foxtail* books, and I loved helping him discover that he is not the man he thought he was. The bachelor rancher is a family man!

At its heart, the *Home to Foxtail* stories have been about characters discovering who they are as children of God. My prayer for you (and for me!) is that we will view ourselves as God does: dearly loved children who are created in His image. No one else's opinion of us matters. Nor does it matter what we may have done in the past. He offers wholeness, healing and peace through the gift of His son, who conquered death that first Easter. Hallelujah!

For more information about epilepsy, there are numerous websites that offer resources, including The Epilepsy Foundation (in the US), www.epilepsy.com.

And if you'd like to learn more about me, please visit my website, www.SusanneDietze.com, where you can also find the recipe for Thatcher and Juniper's Resurrection Cookies.

Thank you for reading!
Susanne